THE CRISIS VECTOR

MITCH HERRON 7

STEVE P. VINCENT

1

Mitch Herron's eyes flickered open and he inhaled sharply. Instinctively, he reached for the pistol he usually kept under his pillow, but his hand only moved a few inches. He tried the other, but it too came up short. Finally, his mind caught up with his muscle memory: he was a prisoner, cable tied to a metal bunk, surrounded by other metal bunks, metal walls, metal closets, and metal footlockers.

"Damn it."

His words attracted the attention of someone outside the door, because a second later there was the shuffle of footsteps and a uniformed U.S. Navy sailor peered inside. Herron locked eyes with the man, a young ensign who looked barely old enough to shave. The sailor didn't acknowledge him, instead ducking back outside and forcing Herron to wait even longer.

With time on his hands, Herron did a mental stocktake. He was groggy, his head hurt like hell, and he was sore all over. Betrayed by an old friend while trying to escape Hong Kong, he was now prisoner aboard a

U.S. Navy ship, with no idea how to get free. Most likely, the ensign was on their way to report to his captor, so he might finally get to see who was in charge.

It wasn't the *most* ideal situation he had ever been in, but it wasn't the worst, either. Before they'd started whaling on him, his captors had said that the U.S. Government wanted a word with him, but Herron had every intention of getting the hell off the ship long before that. Because he was certain that the only thing he'd find back home in America was death.

A few minutes passed before a pair of burly guys dressed all in black arrived at his makeshift prison. One was short and broad, sporting a hefty beard; the other man had less facial hair, was taller and a little younger. He knew their kind. Early in his career, Herron had spent a decade with U.S. Special Forces. On missions all around the world – but mostly in the Middle East – he'd been part of a brotherhood, and this newly arrived pair had the look of members.

It wasn't hard to spot once you knew the signs, and their eyes gave the pair away, the tall one especially sporting a gaze as cold as an Arctic night.

"Morning, guys." Herron grinned, trying to get under their skin. "Which outfit you with?"

They didn't answer. Instead, Cold Eyes trained a pistol on him while Beardy went to work cutting the cable ties that bound Herron's hands and feet to the bed.

The second he was free, Herron mustered all the power he could and shoved Beardy back into Cold Eyes. The stout operative staggered back a step or two, enough to stymie his partner's aim, costing him a clean shot.

That was all Herron needed.

He kicked out at the leg Beardy had planted to balance himself, a brutal strike aimed at the knee. The joint collapsed, driving a grunt of pain from a hard man, who fell to the ground. Herron finished the job with a hard kick to the head, enough to knock the guy out but probably not to kill him. He had no great desire to kill U.S. military personnel unless they made him.

Cold Eyes had regained his balance and once again had his pistol up, but Herron's hunch was that the pair were under orders *not* to shoot him. That gave him a chance. He gripped Cold Eyes' gun hand at the wrist, trying to wrench the weapon free and take it himself, but the other man resisted with serious strength and technique.

"I may not be able to shoot you..." Cold Eyes' voice was a disinterested monotone as he dodged a quick jab Herron threw at his head. "But I can still hurt you."

He caught Herron's hand, squeezed and then bent the joint up so hard it forced him to go down onto one knee to stop his wrist from breaking. He cried out, and tried to punch at Cold Eyes' midsection with his other fist, but his captor had a significant size and reach advantage. Herron did land a few blows, but they landed like the pitter-patter of rain against a window.

A hammer blow rocked him, taking him right on the jaw and leaving him reeling. A second later Cold Eyes let go of his wrist: the force of the blow and the loss of the one thing holding him up was a double whammy, sending Herron sprawling.

A brutal kick took him in the ribs, smashing the breath from him, then another and another, keeping him down on the floor and unable to get back into the fight. It was the same kind of beating you'd find in any bar across America on a bad night. And then it was over as quickly as it started, when Herron had expected the beating to continue.

"That's enough," Cold eyes said. "You get to live, because one of my superiors decided they need you for a job."

Cold Eyes had done just enough to put him down, then backed off – the sign of a calm professional.

Which wasn't a good sign for Herron's escape prospects.

* * *

HERRON WAS ONCE AGAIN RESTRAINED. This time, to a chair in some out-of-the-way corner of the ship, waiting for whoever was pulling the string of Cold Eyes and his crew to show up. He'd been waiting an hour or so, still smarting from the short and sharp beating he'd taken, which had done more harm to his pride than his body, but had given him a level of respect for the men babysitting him.

He didn't know who they were, but he'd bet his ass they were tier one operators.

Finally, the door of the small room opened and admitted a small army of people into the room. Most were special forces operators like Cold Eyes – half a dozen of them – but one man stood out from the rest. He was small, clean-shaven, and sharply dressed in a business suit, the polar opposite of the other men.

A *suit.*

He stepped closer to Herron and crouched down so

he was at eye level. "Mr Herron, I trust these men are giving you the hospitality you so richly deserve."

Herron sneered. "I could do with a steak and a cold beer, but the reception has been better than I expected when you scooped me up in Hong Kong."

The suited man shrugged. "I'm not sure you realise quite how lucky you are to be alive, Mr Herron. I'd originally asked these fine men here to shoot you on sight."

"So what changed?"

"As so often appears to be the case with you, Mr Herron, something came up at the last minute that requires your particular brand of carnage."

"Surprised anything comes up for a man your age..."

The Suit gave a thin smirk, then he took a step back and nodded at Cold Eyes. "Sergeant Bradshaw..."

Cold Eyes – Bradshaw – nodded, stepped forward and delivered a shot to the side of Herron's head, enough to snap his head around. "Behave."

Herron shook his head, trying to recover, then locked eyes on Bradshaw. "I'm really looking forward to the day we can have a fair fight..."

"We had one back when you busted up my buddy's knee." Bradshaw stepped back and leaned against the wall of the room. "You got your ass kicked."

Herron was convinced now that these guys were special forces. They were skilled at the application of violence, but followed their orders to the letter. Any regular grunt would have taken another shot in response to the insult, but Bradshaw had shrugged it off and deferred to the Suit.

With the message sent, the Suit stepped forward again. "I'll cut to the chase. Your first option is to board a helicopter, fly to Gitmo, and spend the rest of your days alongside the self-proclaimed warlords."

Herron said nothing.

"Your *other* option is to board a helicopter, fly to the States and complete a mission I assign to you – with Bradshaw and his boys along for the ride."

"And once I do?"

"You'll have done something useful before you die." The Suit let the words hang heavy. "The job is critical to national security and there's nobody else who has both the skills and deniability to do it."

"You guys must be desperate," Herron scoffed. "But you're not doing a great job selling it. How come I still end up dead at the end?"

"Because on no less than a dozen occasions you've compromised American national security yourself," the Suit replied. "And I think we all know a bullet in the head is preferable to life in a small cage in Cuba."

Herron had spent his share of time imprisoned, first in Fiji and then in China, and he had no desire to rot away slowly in custody. Still, no matter how exhausted he was after going toe-to-toe with the government of the People's Republic of China over the past few years, he had no great passion for a useless death.

"I'll happily die for the right cause, but I don't think you're offering me anything noble..." Herron's voice trailed off. He waited until the Suit nodded, then continued. "So how about I do your job and you let me live?"

The Suit's response was instant. "Absolutely not. We know you had the same deal on the table with China and went rogue, so our terms are simple. Do the job, eat a bullet, and let Erica Kearns continue with her life."

Herron's eyes narrowed. It had been a long time since he'd heard his benefactor's name, the woman who'd helped him foil the Omega Strain and overcome the Enclave. The woman he'd had to leave behind. When he'd fled America, he'd known he'd never see Kearns again, but he'd hoped he'd done enough to keep her safe in his absence. Now the Suit was here to dash that hope.

"We have evidence Ms Kearns abetted a known terrorist and one of the FBI's top 20 most wanted people," he went on.

"Me."

"Precisely."

"Then why isn't she behind bars already?"

"We thought there might come a time when we needed leverage against you. Take it as a compliment."

"So I do the job, you kill me, and then you leave Kearns alone?" Herron studied the Suit's face, trying to read his intentions, but his captor remained expressionless. "Okay, sign me up."

* * *

THE HELICOPTER CAME into land at an airfield somewhere on the western seaboard of the United States. Herron had tried and failed to guess which one, based on the small geographic markers he'd been able to spot during the night- flight; neither the pilots nor Bradshaw and the other special forces babysitters had said a word about their destination.

America had a lot of military bases and even more civilian airfields. He could be anywhere.

Not that it mattered much. The Suit had enough

over Herron to keep him on the straight and narrow. He owed Erica Kearns a lot, so unless the mission was a completely unthinkable atrocity, he'd do what he was told. Then he'd die, leaving her to live out her life in the relative peace he'd almost shattered for her a half-dozen times.

Since agreeing to the Suit's demands, Herron had been treated totally differently by Bradshaw and his men. They'd cut his restraints, dragged him to his feet and then escorted him through the bowels of the ship to the infirmary. There, a navy medic had tended to his ailments, asking no questions as she did.

Now he was ready to work.

He had been given nothing but a clean set of clothes – all black – and five minutes to shower, after which they'd boarded the chopper. Bradshaw and his squad were all sporting tactical rigs, night-vision gear, their choice of primary weapon, and holstered sidearms.

Yet, despite their cool demeanour, Herron could sense the tension in them, small signals he had grown accustomed to spotting: the tightness around the corners of their eyes, the way they gripped their weapons, the clipped manner in which they spoke to each other over the helicopter's onboard comms system.

It was like they were already on a mission and the action could fire up at any minute.

"What's got you guys so on edge?" Herron asked Bradshaw. He needed to make peace with the man if he was going to work with him and his team. "Can you tell me what I'm walking into here?"

"Technically, you're flying..." Bradshaw's voice remained serious despite the joke, which eased none of the tension, earning nothing even resembling a laugh from the others. "We know what you did to foil both the British and the Chinese attempts to control you, so we're going to play it smarter than that and make sure you know what you need to know, when you need to know it."

"Got it," Herron said, bitterness in his voice as he sat back in his chair. He had even less control over his own future now than when he'd woken up handcuffed to a steel bunk.

He stewed on the thought, even as the helicopter banked and descended toward a cluster of brightly coloured lights. The scene looked like many other airfields Herron had approached at night, and he tried to soak in as much detail as possible, his brain processing all the input. But even as the pilot touched the helicopter down gently and a pair of ground crew rushed in to open the side doors, he still did not know his location.

As soon as the doors were open, two of Bradshaw's men exited through each door, weapons raised and searching for threats. That was curious to Herron; he saw no reason to expect hostiles at a U.S. airfield. Alone now on the chopper with Bradshaw, two other remaining operatives and the pilot. Herron reached down to unbuckle his harness. He didn't get the chance, Bradshaw slamming his palm against his chest.

"I just want to make it clear one more time." He leaned in real close to Herron. "This is my operation and you're a cog in my machine, got it?"

"Got it," Herron replied, resisting the urge to break his arm. "I'll do what I need to do to keep my friend out of trouble, then I'll shoot myself in the head if that's what you want."

"Oh, no..." Bradshaw laughed. "If there's one thing I *definitely* want after the shit you pulled with my guy's knee, it's to shoot you in the head myself."

"Can I trust the guy in the suit to live up to his end of the bargain and leave my friend alone?"

"Hell if I know, but what choice do you have?"

Herron waited for more, but no more came. Instead, Bradshaw took his hand off Herron and exited the chopper with his pair of remaining comrades. Nobody seemed concerned Herron was left alone with the pilot, that he might overpower them and steal the bird, because everyone knew if he did Erica Kearns would spend her life behind bars.

As he unbuckled his harness to follow the others out, he heard the pilot grunt. Shaking himself free of the harness, he turned in his seat to look: there was a hole in the windshield, and the pilot was slumped forward, missing a quarter of his skull.

Herron dived to the floor of the chopper, trying to conceal himself from the shooter. His mind raced. This should have been a secure environment...

Keeping low, he risked a look outside. A second later, the world beyond the chopper was filled with noise and light: flames and muzzle flashes, gunshots and explosions. Whoever was hitting the airport – or just this aircraft – was doing it with a hell of a lot more than a single sniper.

What the hell had he gotten himself into?

2

———

Keeping low, Herron moved out of the chopper and into the chaos engulfing the airport. He took cover behind the landing strut – imperfect protection, but better than nothing – and took stock of everything that was happening. As he took in the surrounding scene, he wished he'd chosen the door that led to Gitmo.

Bradshaw and his crew had fanned out from the chopper and were taking heavy fire. One of them was down on the tarmac, but the others had made it to firing positions behind refuelling tankers and other helicopters. Both members of the ground crew Herron had seen approaching the bird when they'd first landed were dead; if he had to guess, they had been the original ambush crew and had seriously underestimated the guys aboard the chopper.

Further out, concealed shooters were pouring on automatic fire, only their muzzle flashes revealing their location amongst the inky darkness. Herron guessed there were at least ten foes firing at them, plus at least one sniper who'd taken down the pilot. Bradshaw had five guys – one of them down already – and Herron, who was weaponless and lacking night vision gear.

"Is this thing still working?" Herron asked over the headset he'd been given to communicate with the team aboard the chopper. He was met with silence, which meant Bradshaw's team had likely shifted to a secure channel to coordinate their actions. "Damn it."

The first bullets ricocheted off the metal frame of the landing struts, and, thinking fast, he burst into a run. He angled himself toward the member of Bradshaw's team who'd bought it, knowing he was terribly exposed in no-man's-land, but that this was his best chance to get in the fight.

He expected to be downed by one of the shooters at any second – or by Bradshaw's team, mistaking him for a hostile. But standing around in the middle of a firefight with your finger up your ass was a recipe to get shot; this way, at least he'd die trying.

Miraculously, no hot lead slammed into him, and he slid down low onto the tarmac next to the downed operative. Using the corpse as cover, he started stripping the operative of the gear he needed – his suppressed submachine gun, his sidearm, and his tactical helmet, which housed night-vision goggles and comms gear.

Herron would finally be able to see, hear, and communicate.

All the while, the two sides swapped gunfire, the airfield a war zone. Herron lay prone, continuing to use the dead man as a shield, and lowered the night vision goggles over his eyes. The four-lens rig immediately lit up the night, clearly showing what was happening.

It wasn't pretty.

At least a half dozen enemy shooters were concealed on the far side of the tarmac, pouring fire towards Bradshaw, Herron and the others. Some were hiding amongst the terminal's small buildings, others were huddled behind fences or vehicles. He could spot at least one who'd had been taken down, but there was still a hell of a lot more work to do.

For their part, Bradshaw and his crew were doing their best to return fire from far less secure cover; no matter how skilled they were, the situation was bleak. Herron had to change the arithmetic – fast – or they'd all be overrun. He let loose a tight, accurate burst of fire, dropping one ambusher.

There was no time to plan properly, he'd have to make something up on the fly.

"This is Herron," he said into the headset, hoping Bradshaw and the others could hear and would listen. "I'm going to make a break for their positions, but I'll need some covering fire to help get me there."

"Put that weapon down and get off the network!" Bradshaw's voice boomed in Herron's earpiece. "You are not authorised to possess a weapon!"

"Being shot at is all the authorisation I need." Herron drilled another one of the unidentified enemy shooters. "Tango down!"

There was a long pause on the comms, during which both groups of shooters — Herron included — continued to spray rounds at each other. Another of Bradshaw's men dropped, his cry of pain clearly audible in between the gunfire.

That sealed the deal.

"Try not to get your ass shot off," Bradshaw said. His tone suggested he was speaking against his better judgement, lacking any other choice. "But you're giving me that weapon if we make it out of this."

"Deal."

Swiftly, Herron outlined his plan, one skilled operator to another, improvising a strategy. Then, they executed it.

The warning cries came first, barked out over comms.

"Frag out!"

"Frag out!"

The grenades were impossible to see in the darkness, even with the aid of night-vision equipment. Herron had to hope Bradshaw's guys had decent arms, or else he'd never make it to the enemy lines without getting shot to bits. But, a second later, he wasn't disappointed.

The grenades detonated amongst the enemy, one shooter crying out in pain as he fell. With the others forced to keep their heads down, Herron climbed to his feet and burst into a run, Bradshaw's team unloading bursts of full-auto gunfire, burning through their ammunition at an alarming rate in order to keep Herron and his plan alive.

The torrent of gunfire forming a bass backing track to his footfalls, Herron closed the distance to the nearest point of enemy control: an ambulance parked on the edge of the tarmac. He got there intact, sheltering behind the engine block on the far side from the shooters, just as the volley of fire from Bradshaw's men eased. They were running out of ammo.

Herron dropped prone. Peering under the ambulance, he saw the feet of one of the enemy operatives; he didn't seem to know Herron was so close by. Either the guy was an idiot, a rookie, or the covering fire had kept his head down far better than Herron had dared hope. Whichever, he was a dead man.

Herron aimed at his legs and fired. Immediately, the man's screams filled the gaps in sound between gunshots. He fell to the tarmac in agony, and Herron fired again, a double tap to the man's face, putting him out of his misery. It was a good start, but Herron knew he had a long way to go if he was going to get them out of this mess.

He climbed back to his feet and rounded the ambulance, his keen eyes searching for another target. All the while, Bradshaw's team kept shooting and funnelling intelligence to him over the comms network. Herron already respected their skills, given they'd foiled both his escape aboard the ship and the ambush upon exiting the helo, but with each update, he gained more appreciation for the tactical acumen of the team.

Now it was time to show them what he could do.

He changed out his magazine, then got to work. After killing the man by the ambulance, he wasn't sure if the would-be assassins had figured out he was amongst them, but he was determined to cause chaos and confusion now he was in amongst them.

Moments ago, the ambushers had possessed the initiative.

Now they had surrendered it and were fighting a battle on two fronts.

He keyed his comms. "Bradshaw, I'm near the ambulance, check fire."

"Confirmed." Bradshaw replied. "You've got two shooters right near you, inside the terminal building."

The airstrip where they had landed was hardly LAX,

and the terminal building to serve passengers at the small airport was a simple, single-storey structure. Despite that, Herron couldn't see a single shooter, let alone two. He would have headed in that direction momentarily; either Bradshaw had saved him from a nasty ambush or he was walking him into one.

"Bradshaw, confirm two contacts inside the terminal building adjacent to my position?"

"Confirmed. The second you approach they're going to see you so we'll hit it with covering fire on your mark."

Still unsure if he could trust the operative, Herron said, "Aim high. I don't want to eat a stray. Three, two, one, mark."

He hesitated a second longer than he normally would, watching as fresh gunfire pounded the terminal building, shattering glass and pockmarking the walls. Then he raised his weapon and headed through the main door in from the tarmac. Helped by his night-vision equipment in the otherwise dark building, he instantly saw a pair of shooters huddled down near the corner.

It took less than a second to aim and fire, cutting down one of the shooters then the other. It was a fearsome display of controlled violence against two targets who never even knew he was there, but there were still more enemies to contend with before he could feel too happy with himself.

He shifted his aim and swept the rest of the small building. There was a handful of tables and chairs, where passengers could wait for their upcoming flight, but no threats; nor were there any behind the counter of the small cafeteria, the only other feature the building contained. He made a quick check of the bathroom, and found nothing.

Almost as an afterthought, he moved toward the two downed shooters and fired a single shot into the head of each. He would not risk leaving hostiles in his wake. Quickly, he stripped the bodies of several magazines he could use, as well as a pair of flashbang grenades that might come in handy.

"Terminal clear," he said, updating his team. "What's the situation, Bradshaw?"

"More trouble headed your way from the south – a leaker we didn't have time to take down after we spotted him."

Herron's eyes widened and he spun one-eighty degrees. A man was entering the building, his weapon searching for targets as Herron's had a moment ago. Herron hit the deck right as gunfire filled the terminal.

"Shit!" Herron cursed, scrambling along the ground for cover. That he'd let an enemy get the jump on him was a sign he'd lost some of his sharpness while gallivanting around the Pacific. "Get your head in the game, Mitch."

As Herron chided himself, the shooter kept advancing, firing single shots to keep his head down until he could manoeuvre into a sight line and end the battle. Herron wasn't confident he could pop up, aim and fire faster than the shooter could blow his head off. The gunman probably had body armour, whereas Herron had nothing but a metal table for protection.

But Herron's edge on a battlefield wasn't his ability to shoot. Sure, he could do that well, but so could plenty of others.

His edge was that he could *think*.

Quickly.

Herron raised his night-vision goggles and then reached for the flashbang grenades he'd appropriated. As the single shots exploded against the tough metal table, Herron pulled the pin and popped the safety handle on each flashbang. Closing his eyes, he lobbed them over his cover and into the area where he estimated the shooter would be.

"Banger out!" Herron announced to Bradshaw and his team, doubting they were in the vicinity but following good discipline with his impromptu allies anyway. Then he closed his eyes and covered his ears.

The flashbangs exploded a split-second apart, disorienting Herron a little despite his precautions. His vision – even with his eyes closed – danced with colour, his ears rang, and his head felt like it'd been punched a few times, but he didn't have the luxury of a lengthy recovery if he was going to prevail.

What he had was enough training to help him shake off the effects a little faster than most people, including his opponent. When he replaced his night-vision gear over his eyes, stood and aimed at the shooter, it was barely a fair fight: his foe was on his knees, dazed and with little control of his senses. A sitting duck.

The man's head exploded from Herron's perfectly aimed shot, his senses destroyed far more permanently than from any flashbang. As he dropped to the ground, silence descended. Both Bradshaw's crew and the ambushers had stopped firing – one side or the other had been wiped out.

Herron keyed his comms. "Sitrep?"

"It's done." Bradshaw sounded tired. "For now."

Herron exhaled slowly and headed back towards the

helicopter, exhausted, covered in blood and starving. He held his borrowed gun loosely by his side, alert in case some other threat emerged but not wanting to get pegged by one of Bradshaw's crew as he approached.

Any danger of that lessened when Bradshaw broke off from the rest of his men – who fanned out to take up defensive positions – and moved in Herron's direction. "Nice shooting."

Herron simply nodded. "There could be more of them inbound. Are you sure the perimeter is secure?"

"Nothing is secure in the States right now," Bradshaw admitted. "But if they had more assets in the area, they would have thrown them at us. They clearly knew we were bringing in a special package."

"Me?" Herron raised an eyebrow, then laughed when Bradshaw nodded. "Been a while since I got that sort of attention. At least three weeks."

"Well, you better be as good as advertised, because this warm-up act just cost one of my guys his life."

Herron nodded and then placed his weapon back on the corpse of Bradshaw's downed man. Some pencil pusher would no doubt need to account for it. "Who were those guys? And why are they attacking us on US soil?"

Bradshaw shook his head. "What the hell, I figure you've earned some honesty. They were us. SOCOM."

Herron looked at him in disbelief. He'd been part of Special Operations Command prior to his career as a solo assassin. In that time, he'd have died for his comrades, and they'd have died for him without question – to hear the guys who'd been shooting at them should have been friendly raised a lot of questions. However, it also answered one: if SOCOM were shooting at each other, it made sense that the Suit needed *external* help.

"All right. Why are SOCOM shooting at us?"

"We're not totally sure yet. Around a week ago, whole bunches of people who should be loyal to the country started acting against it. It's hard to know who's a friendly and who's a hostile right now."

Herron winced. It would be impossible to work in any national security role if you didn't have confidence in the people, systems and structures around you. "So who do you think is behind it?"

"We think they're Chinese sleeper cells causing trouble before China makes a play for Taiwan. Nobody else has the combination of capability and motivation."

A giant piece of the puzzle fell into place for Herron. Over the last year, he'd tangled with the interests of the Chinese Government three times: in Fiji, the Philippines, and Hong Kong. China's efforts were those of a country trying to muscle its way to prominence, dominating its neighbours and seizing territory it considered its own.

But Taiwan was different.

An island only miles off the coast of China, it had long been regarded by the mainland as a rebel breakaway province. But nearly a century since the nationalist government had fled to the island after a civil war against the communists, Taiwan had flourished into a vibrant democracy and modern economy. That, combined with its highly strategic location in the South China Sea and its semiconductor industry, had attracted other powers to support it.

None more so than America.

The United States had long had a policy of strategic

ambiguity towards Taiwan, neither confirming nor denying that American troops would fight to defend the island. That policy had stayed China's hand for a long time, but if Bradshaw was right that hesitation was no longer a factor. Increasingly belligerent, China might try its luck, fomenting unrest and causing enough trouble among America's crack troops to keep them at home.

Suddenly, a mission Herron had accepted blindly to keep Erica Kearns safe had taken on another, even more personal dimension. The faces of the friends he'd met over the last year in the places he'd pushed back against China flashed across his mind; some were allies who were no longer alive, and some who were but would never be the same.

"We need to stop them," Herron said. "But I want to know what makes you guys above reproach."

Bradshaw's face clouded over and his hands balled into fists. "What makes my guys above board – including the one who died trying to protect your ass – is a history of successful mission activity hostile to the PRC. The higher ups think – and I agree – that it seems unlikely China would employ such assets to cause trouble."

"Fair," Herron said, conceding the point. "So have I earned the right to know what the mission is? Because I'm on board with anything that will mess with the Chinese Government. There's more to this, or the Suit would have saved me all the secrecy and told me all this back on the ship. I want it straight."

Bradshaw nodded. "Fine. The sleeper cell – or cells, plural, we're not sure how many – are gunning for the Director of National Intelligence and it's your job to stop him going *splat*."

3

"Home sweet home." Herron looked out the window of the beat-up old sedan he and Bradshaw were riding in. "You sure this is the right address?"

"I told you we'd be going off-grid," Bradshaw replied, although his voice suggested he was toeing the company line rather than really believing it. "We'll only be here a few days."

The house looked like the set from a post-apocalyptic movie, a squat structure with peeling paint and several broken windows. Out front, a rusted car sat atop the dirt and weeds that passed for a lawn; at the end of the driveway was a letterbox overstuffed with junk mail, the number painted on it confirming to Herron they were exactly where they were meant to be.

The journey hadn't been a long one. As soon as the Suit had managed to whistle up a light aircraft for them, they'd cleared out of the compromised airport, which Herron had learned was near San Francisco. It had taken an hour, during which Herron, Bradshaw and the rest of the team had formed a defensive perimeter and hoped like hell for no more fireworks.

Less than five minutes after the plane had landed, they'd been in the air again. This time, Herron had been told where they were headed: McCarran International Airport in Las Vegas, Nevada. Herron could think of worse places to complete a last mission before he took a bullet in the head...

... like the house they'd just arrived at.

"*This* place is *our headquarters* for that *really important mission* to save the DNI?"

Herron felt it was a fair question. The Director of National Intelligence was the most important position in the United States intelligence establishment: a member of the President's cabinet and the executive ultimately in charge of the entire intelligence community. Every important overseas military or intelligence operation undertaken by the United States had input from the DNI.

To lose him on the eve of a crisis between China and Taiwan would be catastrophic.

Bradshaw shifted the car into park and engaged the handbrake. "It's too risky to go to a normal U.S. Intelligence safe house. You saw how well landing at the military base went..."

"Sure, but we couldn't just stay at a Best Western?" Herron asked. "You had to pick the slum house?"

Bradshaw ignored him, so Herron conceded the point. He popped the door and exited the vehicle, the oppressive Nevada heat hitting him full in the face. As Bradshaw also climbed out of their vehicle, the rest of the spec ops crew pulled up in second and third cars. The other four survivors of the ambush at the airfield got out of their rides, and Herron couldn't help but smirk as they voiced their opinions about the accommodation.

"Shithole..."

"I joined the military to get *away* from shit like this..."

"I hope the rats are tasty..."

Bradshaw took the griping from his guys better than he took it from Herron. "I know it's not much to write home about, but we can't be sure the usual sites aren't compromised. I got in touch with a buddy in Las Vegas P.D. to hook us up with this place. The owner is locked up, so we won't be disturbed and we'll be off the radar."

He gestured for everyone to follow him inside, and Herron let the rest of the crew go first. As he approached the front door, he looked around, scoping the neighbourhood for any sort of threat. It looked like the perfect location for a hideaway, every house in the street looking as derelict as this one and not one other person in sight. Just the sort of no-questions-asked-or-answered place they needed to lie low.

Inside, the living room had a half-dozen field cots, set up before their arrival, while in the kitchen there were boxes of food. The best part came when they reached the bedroom at the back of the house.

"Once I hooked up the place, the Suit saw we'd be well catered for." Bradshaw said, smiling as he held his arm out like a game show host revealing a grand prize. "Pick your poison."

The bedroom had no furniture, but it *did* have a dozen large duffel bags and the same number of gun cases. It was the most gear Herron had seen in one place since he'd fled America several years ago. He stayed back while the rest of the team got amongst it, replacing what they'd expended during the battle for the airfield or otherwise changing out what they already had. There were rifles, submachine guns, sidearms, body armour, an assortment of grenades, and comms gear. As always, each operator had a slightly different set of preferences for their fit-out, which was a central feature of many of the elite squads in the United States military.

Herron was no different.

When the others were done, he grabbed one of the duffel bags, emptied it onto the floor, then filled it up again with his chosen tools of the trade. He focused on getting a wide enough range of equipment that he could complete most missions – a necessity, given he didn't quite know the nature of the threat he might face.

First, he stuffed the bag with heavy-duty gear – a suppressed submachine gun with a red-dot sight, a suppressed pistol for close-in work, and a combat knife. Next, he put in body armour with plates, grenades and magazines, and a tactical rig to carry it all.

The whole time he worked, Bradshaw was leaning against the doorframe, watching him. Herron didn't care – he figured he'd be under close surveillance until the job was done. "No helmets? No night vision?"

Bradshaw shook his head. "Won't need either where we're going."

"And you're not going to tell me where that is?"

When Bradshaw didn't respond, Herron turned back to the arsenal, doing a mental stock take to make sure he'd covered all the possible bases. At last, he hefted the bag and turned to Bradshaw. "When does the mission start?"

"That's up to you." Bradshaw pushed himself off the door frame. "Follow me."

* * *

THE STINK that overwhelmed him as he descended into the basement of the house was part body-odour, part rotten food, part piss, part shit, and part vomit. It was a miasma of filth that rankled even a man of Herron's experience, and he coughed and covered his mouth.

Bradshaw hadn't said a word about what they'd find down here, but from the stench it wasn't hard to guess. When the operative flicked on the lights at the top of the staircase, Herron saw more or less what he'd expected.

People in the last act of their life.

The three men were blindfolded, gagged and zip-tied to steel-framed chairs that had been bolted to the ground: a perfect set-up in a makeshift situation. Whoever had imprisoned them here had spent far more time securing the captives than making Bradshaw and his crew comfortable, which made Herron wonder if they were veterans of the extraordinary renditions that routinely took place during the War on Terror.

As well as having their eyes covered, each prisoner wore expensive noise-cancelling headphones, which meant they did not know who or what was in the room with them. They weren't totally passive, however: even with the blindfolds, they were aware a light had been turned on, which catalysed different reactions from each of them.

One, a Chinese guy, looked close to shitting himself again. He was whimpering and trying to speak despite the gag. The underarms of his t-shirt were yellowed with sweat, which told Herron how hot it got down here in the middle of the day, while his pants sported stains of a different kind. He didn't appear to have been tortured or coerced for information, with no visible cuts or bruises: a cleanskin.

The other two were more of a surprise. They were white.

One looked like a pencil pusher, the other had a physique to rival any of Bradshaw's crew, but both were in a similar state to the Chinese guy. The only difference was that these had been through the ringer a little, with bruises and cuts on their faces and arms. Like him, they were mumbling and pulling against their restraints, anxious about what was to come but unable to see or hear anything.

Herron turned to Bradshaw at the top of the stairs. "Who are they and what do we know?"

"Chinese guy is an embassy staffer from D.C. who got scooped up at a local casino; weedy guy is a SOCOM desk jockey caught fucking with shit he shouldn't have been; big guy is a Delta Force soldier with suspect finances. As for what we know: the DNI is on a trip to Vegas from tomorrow. Intel is he'll be targeted then, but we don't know when, where or how."

Herron was taken aback. "We can't just get him to cancel the trip?"

"No," Bradshaw said, exasperated. It seemed the Suit – and others – had probably exhausted their options to achieve just that. "These three are our best shot at answers."

Herron nodded, and Bradshaw stepped back out the door and shut it behind him.

The smell wasn't so bad now Herron was more used to it, and he could focus on what needed to be done. He took a second to strategize, deciding exactly which pimple to pop first – choosing correctly would prevent the need to pop the others – then he took his time removing the blindfolds and the noise-cancelling headphones from each of the captives.

When they could all hear and see, he stood in front of them and said, "I'm here to get answers. I don't care if one or all of you provide them. Those who do will live. Those who don't will die. Here's how it's going to work. You'll all watch – ears covered – as I *talk* with one of you. Once I hear something useful, I'll cover *those* ears and move on to the next one of you. The truth-tellers will live. The liars and the mutes won't."

In response to his words, both Chinese Guy and Desk Jockey were even more scared, but Big Guy looked calm. That told Herron everything he needed to know about where to start with his interrogations. He re-covered the ears of two smaller prisoners, leaving only Big Guy able to hear.

"Look, buddy, I've been in your position: captive and tortured for information." Herron paused, letting the reality of the situation sink in. "Give me what I need."

"Go fuck yourself!" The Big Guy spat at Herron, the gob of sticky saliva falling well short of him.

"Sure you want to do this?"

"Fuck yoursel—"

Herron swung a right hook into the man's jaw. It was an old trick he'd learned: when someone was speaking, their mouth was open and their jaw separated, so a perfectly timed blow would land with a force immense enough to break it. As the Big Guy grunted, and Herron followed up with a left uppercut that snapped his head back, Desk Jockey and Chinese Guy watched, eyes bugged out at the sight.

The Big Guy's whole body was slumped forward, dribbling blood where his chin rested against his chest. He was conscious, but only barely. Meanwhile, Herron's fist was throbbing in agony, but he gave no indication of that fact to the two men watching his every move like a horror movie.

He lifted Big Guy's head up. "Now, do you want to try that again, this time with less cussing and more useful words?"

The man slurred some words – totally indecipherable, thanks to the combination of the broken jaw and the grogginess – but that didn't matter. He could have told Herron the plot to kill the DNI involved six fluffy bunnies and a unicorn; Herron could work with anything. He made a show of asking a few more questions, got a few more gurgled, bullshit responses, then replaced Big Guy's headphones.

Turning to Desk Jockey and Chinese Guy, Herron smiled and looked between them for a long few seconds. Then, he reached around to the back of his pants, pulled out his pistol, and held it by his side. He was certain the pair had noticed the gun in his waistband as he'd been pounding Big Guy, but now it was out and ready for use.

He removed Desk Jockey's headphones. "Your pal there told me everything about the plot to murder the Director of National Intelligence... eventually. So he gets to live. But I'm like a journalist: I need my information verified by two sources. That means it's your turn."

Desk Jockey nodded vigorously and mumbled something incoherent; when Herron removed his gag, he couldn't wait to speak. "Don't hurt me!"

"That's up to you." Herron crossed his arms, the pistol still in his hand. "Tell me where, and when, the attack against the DNI will take place."

"And you'll let me go?" The man's voice was desperate – pleading – but Herron didn't respond. "Fine, they're going to try take him out at the Maxima Casino on Thursday."

Herron nodded, replaced his headphones, and then patted him on the head. Next, he repeated the process with the Chinese Guy, who confirmed the day and location of the attack. The combination of observed violence on another and imminent physical threat worked wonders to open the mouths of people not trained to resist. Herron had seen dozens of terrorists crack under similar tactics.

Now he had what he needed, Herron stuffed the pistol back in the waistband of his pants. After one last glance at Pencil Pusher and Chinese Guy – whose hopeful looks turned fearful as they saw Herron's expression – he headed for the stairs. At the top, he opened the door and saw Bradshaw leaning against the wall, waiting for Herron to finish the job.

"Got what we need?" Bradshaw asked.

Herron nodded.

"Nice work."

"This might be the start of a beautiful friendship," Herron said, deadpan. "I'm going to find some ice for my hand."

"I'll take out the trash, then we can order a pizza,"

Bradshaw said as he drew his pistol and started down the stairs.

HERRON'S EYES opened and adjusted to the darkness. He stayed completely still, listening as Bradshaw and the other operatives slept on the floor nearby. He was surrounded, the crew all grabbing some sleep in the living room, ready to move out and foil the Chinese plot tomorrow. Herron had something else he needed to achieve before then.

The only problem being none of the others could know about it or they'd put a bullet in him on the spot.

He lay there for twenty minutes, alert for any sign that one of the operatives was awake. But, like soldiers all around the world, they were taking advantage of the opportunity to sleep when they could – there was no guarantee about when the next opportunity might come. But that didn't mean one or all of them wouldn't wake at the slightest sound.

Here goes nothing.

He moved whisper-quiet, extracting himself from the embrace of the warm camp cot he'd slumbered in for half the night to stand in the middle of the living room. As he waited for any sign that the slumbering killers surrounding him were stirring, he plotted out his next moves. He had to play it smart, at least until Erica Kearns was safe.

With his eyes adjusted to the darkness, he navigated his way around the sleeping operatives and headed into the kitchen. Amongst the packaging and plastic that remained from dinner, a duffel bag stood in the corner of the room. Herron had seen Bradshaw put it down earlier in the day, filled with guns and other gear for the morning's mission.

He hoped to find something else in there too.

Herron had seen Bradshaw stash his phone after making a call to tell the Suit about the successful interrogation earlier. He slipped his hands into the bag, and a second later, he had found the handset. After tapping the screen to confirm it had battery, he pocketed it.

He crept into the laundry that led from the kitchen, then exited the house through the rear door. Outside, the pale light of the moon illuminated a small backyard, which was no more impressive than the rest of the shithole they were calling home. What it did offer was the chance for a minute of privacy.

Herron made his way to the back of the yard, sat on the ground, and rested his back against the fence. He drew the pistol from his waistband and put it in easy reach on the ground, then took out Bradshaw's phone and unlocked it with the code he'd observed the man using earlier. He took a second to turn the screen brightness down to its lowest setting, then opened a private browser and got Googling.

Erica Kearns was a prominent scientist – a specialist in infectious diseases – but Herron wasn't sure if she'd taken any extra precautions to protect her privacy since their battle against the Enclave. He hoped not, because if he couldn't easily find a way to contact her, all his efforts to get hold of a phone and pry himself out of the trap the Suit had set would be for nothing.

Thankfully, he found her number and immediately dialled it.

A groggy voice answered after a few rings. "Hello? Who is this?"

Herron hesitated; he'd never expected to speak to this woman again. "It's me."

There was an audible intake of breath on the other end of the line. "Mitch?"

"Seen any good movies lately?" He laughed. "It's good to hear your voice."

"I thought you were dead. Then I saw you were imprisoned by the Chinese, and—"

"I'm sorry, I'd love to tell you all about it but there's no time. I'm back in America and I'm being blackmailed."

"Blackmailed..." Her voice trailed off. "Me?"

"You."

Herron gave her a second to digest the news, painfully aware that the longer he stayed on the line, the more risk he ran of being discovered. But while they'd been through a lot together, he wasn't sure how she'd react to being thrust back into danger. Part of the reason he'd left America was to keep her safe. She was the only person he cared about in the whole country, and now, because of him, the gun sights were settled on her again.

"What do you need me to do?" Her voice was filled with the same resolve that had made her the equal of any hard-ass operative. "How can I help you?"

"By disappearing, and not telling me – or anyone else – where you'll be going." He let the words sink in. "Then I can do what needs to be done without fear for your safety if I fail."

She didn't hesitate. "Okay. I trust you, Mitch, and I'll

do what you ask. But how will I know when it's safe to return to my normal life?"

"Go to a public library and set up a Gmail account. Make the username the nickname I gave the first man I killed in your presence, with 12345 on the end. And make the password the name of the restaurant where I last saw you."

Username: Tiny12345@gmail.com

Password: McDonalds

Not even the Suit can have that tracked.

"Okay, I understand," she said.

Herron continued: "Once that's done, send yourself an email with the address of the location you end up hiding, so I can find you once it's safe. I'll come and find you when it's safe to come out of hiding."

"And if you don't?"

"Then it means I'm dead, the threat against you is over, and you can come out of hiding."

"What you *should* have said was that you *will* contact me and that I have nothing to worry about... A few years on your own has clearly done wonders for your social skills, Mitch."

"Guilty as charged, but you should see my tan..." He laughed, trying to reinject some lightness into their conversation, likely the last they'd ever have. "Do you still have some of the cash I gave you when I last saw you?"

"Most of it," she said. "I have a job that pays me plenty, Mitch, and once you told me it was safe to come out of hiding last time I went back to work and didn't need to touch any of the cash."

"Good," he said, relieved she'd have the resources she'd need. "Time to use it now. Don't use your car, your phone, your cards or any of your online accounts once you've sent that email – disappear."

"I understand," she said.

"Last thing," he said. "Don't panic, but you're probably being watched. When you leave your place, dress in baggy clothing, with a hoodie and glasses on at all times. You need to evade the tail the way I showed you."

"Okay," she said. "Are you going to be okay, Mitch?"

Herron was about to respond when he heard the back door of the house open. He pulled the phone down from his ear and locked the screen, his eyes shooting up to identify the threat. He couldn't see who was approaching in the darkness, which he hoped meant the opposite was true – if one of the operatives caught him with a phone, they'd give him a bullet to go with it.

"I know you're out here, motherfucker." Bradshaw's voice penetrated the darkness. "You better be damn convincing when you tell me what you're doing."

Herron ended the call, confident that Bradshaw couldn't see him, then he pocketed the phone and picked up his weapon. "And I've got a pistol aimed at you, so calm down."

"What are you doing out here?" Bradshaw suddenly stepped close enough for Herron to see him.

"I wanted some air and some quiet. You assholes stink and snore. If I wanted to run, I'd be gone, so calm down."

Bradshaw hesitated for a few seconds. "Get the hell back inside and get some sleep. We're moving out in four hours."

4

I f the house Herron had started the day in was the worst place in Nevada, the brand-new Maxima Casino had a solid claim to being the best. Built right in the middle of the Las Vegas Strip, it had been chosen as the venue for a meeting of the heads of intelligence from the Quadrilateral Security Dialogue – the United States, Australia, India and Japan – who were the countries most ready to act in the event of hostility against Taiwan by the People's Republic of China.

Herron doubted if even a fraction of the foot traffic on The Strip knew such a momentous meeting was happening in amongst the gambling and stage shows, but he was certain the government of the PRC did. On the verge of launching their campaign against the breakaway island, they would see the meeting as a tantalising chance to decapitate the most important intelligence figures of all four countries.

Including the DNI.

Dressed in a royal blue suit and mingling with the crowd at the casino entrance, it was Herron's job to stop them. Bradshaw was nearby, similarly decked out, while the rest of the team were dispersed amongst key locations around the Maxima. While they knew the time and place of the attack, thanks to the three bozos in the basement of the derelict house, they didn't know the method, and everyone in the team was on high alert.

Despite that, Herron felt freer than he had in a long time. Now he knew Erica Kearns was on the way to safety, he could do what needed to be done to protect the DNI's life and foil China's ambitions, either by following orders from the Suit and Bradshaw, or freelancing if necessary. Either way, when the job was done, he'd escape if he could, die if he couldn't, safe in the knowledge *she* was out of harm's way.

He whispered into his lapel microphone, outfitted with the rest of the gear at the safe house. "This is Defender Six, I'm still near the entrance in front of the driveway. No sign of trouble."

"Confirmed, Six." Bradshaw's voice boomed in Herron's earpiece. "This is One at the start of the driveway, I got nothing. The DNI is fifteen minutes out, all other Defender elements report."

"This is Two. I've found a nice little sniper's nest overlooking the Strip. I can see the driveway and the entrance to the Maxima."

"Three. I'm between the entrance and the conference facilities. If the DNI gets to me, he should be safe. There's a load of security here and they're not afraid of waving their guns around."

"Four. I've got eyes on the conference area and can confirm Three's assessment – there's a shit-ton of security and police here, too."

Any of whom could draw and put a bullet in our guy...

"This is Five, available in reserve for anyone who needs me."

"Stay sharp." Bradshaw said. "If we lose the DNI today, we're probably going to war blind in the next few days."

Not me... I'll probably be dead.

Banishing the thought, Herron focused back on the entrance. Despite the team's capability – and his own – they lacked the numbers to fully defend as tightly as they'd like. And a killer could reveal themselves at any moment to take a shot at the DNI.

Around a quarter-hour later, Herron spotted the DNI's convoy of vehicles turning off the Strip and into the casino's circular driveway. There were four Chevy Suburbans in total, two in front of and two behind the vehicle that had carried the DNI the short distance from McCarran International Airport. The cars were being guided in by motorcycle police with lights flashing.

Herron reached into his pocket and gripped his pistol. He carried it in a leg holster, a hole he'd cut out of the inside of his suit pocket giving him access to the weapon. "I have eyes on the motorcade."

"He's in an armoured vehicle, so there shouldn't be any risk until he's outside of the car..." It seemed to Herron Bradshaw didn't sound *totally* sure about that. "If shit goes down, we get him inside, no matter what."

Herron watched the convoy approach and then come to a stop. The DNI emerged from the vehicle, surrounded by a small army of protective agents. Although his detail clearly wanting to get him inside as fast as possible, he was an old man and walked slowly – painfully slowly – toward the entrance.

"This is Defender Two," said Bradshaw's man in the sniper perch. "He's a sitting duck down there…"

As if on cue, three bystanders reached inside their coats.

"Shooters!" Herron declared, simultaneously drawing his own pistol. "Take them out, Two!"

The sniper put a shot into each of the would-be assassins faster than any of them could aim at the DNI. But as they dropped, Herron kept his attention on the protective detail, as well as the private security and cops nearby. Most were surrounding the DNI, focused on getting him inside, but a pair of cops were behaving weirdly, standing off the pack with their guns drawn as if waiting for something else to happen.

Then a pair of cops started shooting into the DNI's protective detail.

"Oh shit…" Herron cried. "Some cops are hostile!"

He raised his pistol and downed one of the rogue cops, even as Defender Two took down the other. They were too late to help the half-dozen agents who'd been cut down in the exchange, however; some writhed in pain on the ground in front of the casino, others were lay motionless. The remaining agents focused on returning the DNI to his vehicle, abandoning their plans to get him inside the casino given the cops were now gunning for them.

"Good shooting Two and Six," Bradshaw said, relieved. "They're bugging out, so it looks like job done. Everyone fold in on Two."

Herron kept watch as the surviving bodyguards bundled the DNI into his vehicle, a few of the loyal agents jumping in with him. They sped away a moment later, two more agents jumping into one of the Chevy Suburbans and following – a much smaller convoy, moving much faster than before.

Foiling the attack had taken only seconds, but Herron doubted Bradshaw's belief that it was all over. In his experience with the Chinese Government, they rarely gave up if their first attempt failed, and he wouldn't be surprised if there were many more angles of attack.

His fears were immediately confirmed as two sedans rammed through the police barricade outside the Maxima's driveway, scattering the police officers manning the post. The cars got on the tail of the DNI's motorcade, automatic gunfire erupting from their windows. Dozens of rounds pounded the chase car, forcing it off the road.

Herron broke into a run toward one of the Chevy Suburbans abandoned by the DNI's protectors. "Six moving to intercept! One, get ready to jump in!"

He floored the gas, racing to the end of the driveway where Bradshaw was positioned. It would take precious seconds for the team leader to jump aboard, but Herron would need the extra pair of hands to have the best chance to stop the sedans.

Bradshaw flung open the passenger door and climbed in, Herron speeding up the moment he was inside. "Hope you know what you're doing..."

Herron cursed as he tapped the brakes, then jerked the wheel to the left, cutting into the left lane and avoiding a build-up of traffic outside the Bellagio. "I'd kill for a siren right now."

"We've got guns..." Bradshaw replied, winding down

his window and firing a full auto burst from his submachine gun into the air. "Next best thing."

Herron gripped the wheel tight, zig-zagging in and out of traffic at breakneck speed. Some cars up ahead *responded* to Bradshaw's gunfire, clearing out of the way, and making it marginally easier to gain ground on the vehicles up ahead, but there was still no guarantee Herron and Bradshaw would make it before the DNI was run off the road.

"Reloading!" Bradshaw spoke from beside Herron, slamming a fresh magazine into his submachine gun. "Need a new mag?"

"Sure," Herron said. He was busy enough with the driving, but he'd never turn down the comfort of a fully loaded pistol. "Then call the Suit and make sure he tells those agents with the DNI that we're friendlies!"

Engine roaring, Herron's Suburban performed well, but they still had a lot of ground to make up. The casinos that made up the Strip whizzed by... then the DNI's vehicle veered off the main drag. All the while, Bradshaw got on the phone to the Suit.

Herron flung the Suburban into the same turn. "They're headed for the airport. They got enough men there to shoot the hell out of a few carloads of traitors?"

"Hell if I know," Bradshaw said. "But we were ordered to keep the DNI safe, so our place is on that tarmac until we're *certain* he is."

Herron nodded and kept the vehicle at its top speed, an easier feat now they were off the busier parts of the Strip. The airport was only a few minutes away, but it was long enough that more cop cars could arrive, lights flashing and sirens wailing. By the time they reached the VIP gate to the tarmac hosting the DNI's jet, a massive convoy of law enforcement was riding to the rescue.

None of that did a thing to reduce the danger: the assassins had come prepared. Out on the open spaces of the tarmac, the sedans pulled out wide to drive on either side of the DNI's vehicle, keeping about twenty yards clear of it. Herron watched, confused by the move... until he spotted as the tip of a rocket-propelled grenade appearing through the window of one car.

"They're going to crack open the car with an RPG!"

Bradshaw shook his head. "They'll fry themselves with the backblast inside the sedan..."

"They won't. RPGs have a two-stage rocket."

Bradshaw's eyes narrowed, then widened. "Fuck!"

"Take the wheel and give me your gun."

Bradshaw did as asked, and Herron lowered the driver's side window. He angled his body so that he was hanging out while still keeping his foot on the gas and aimed the submachine gun at the sedan. Using the window frame to steady himself, he fired a full auto burst, desperately hoping to disrupt the imminent weapon launch.

"Come on..." Herron snarled as shots blossomed on the back of the sedan, sparking against the metal near the back wheels. "Come on!"

As his gun clicked dry, the RPG fired... and one of the rear tires on the sedan blew out. The car spun, the driver losing traction at such high speeds, and Herron held his breath as the rocket closed the distance to the DNI's vehicle. It was a close call, but the last-second movement of the car had done enough to louse up the shot. The rapidly moving projective flew right over the top of the DNI's vehicle, impacting the terminal building instead.

"Yes!" Herron cheered as he leaned back into the car.

"Don't get too excited," Bradshaw said. "Looks like their pals are tooled up the same…"

While the first sedan lost ground – and would soon be swarmed by cops – an RPG was emerging from the window of the second, still keeping pace with the DNI. With the car farther away and on the wrong side of his own vehicle to be able to aim reliably, Herron knew he couldn't get lucky enough to make the same shot twice.

Thankfully, the DNI's driver was a quick thinker. Suddenly he changed course and veered directly *toward* the assassins.

Herron grinned, wondering if the driver was a veteran – only a veteran or someone with a very specific interest in Russian rocket launchers would know they needed a minimum range of about 20 yards.

"If he can get close enough, the rocket won't do shit," Herron said, resuming control of the vehicle. He tossed his empty weapon to Bradshaw. "Reload everything we've got, we might need it in a second or two."

He kept the nose of his vehicle aimed right at the sedan, closing on it painfully slowly, every vehicle in the chase roaring at full speed. As he did, the DNI's vehicle nosed closer to the sedan, making sure the rocket launcher didn't have the distance it needed to work.

Up ahead, the DNI's plane loomed ever closer, by now the agents near to it also firing on the sedan.

Running out of options, the assassin shifted aim and fired the RPG at them instead.

The rocket closed the distance in a second,

exploding in a small fireball, cutting down the protection detail.

"They're going to need to put out some recruiting ads," Bradshaw said, deadpan, as he took in the carnage – a dispassionate special forces veteran unmoved by bloodshed. "Guns are ready."

Herron nodded, held out his hand, and Bradshaw slapped his freshly reloaded pistol into his palm. He placed the piece in his lap and shifted his foot off the gas: the sedan and the DNI's vehicle had started to slow the closer they got to the plane.

Herron jerked the wheel and slammed the brakes, swerving the big Suburban so it was side-on to the now stationary sedan. From the passenger seat, Bradshaw aimed his submachine gun and opened fire, along with every other agent and cop within range. Herron took a second to bundle out of the vehicle, scooted the short distance to the hood and then opened fire with his pistol, using the engine block for cover.

He unloaded a full clip into the sedan, his shots and those from the law-enforcement officers punching deep welts into the vehicle. The car's windows shattered, its tires were blown to bits, and its panels were riddled by a thousand high-velocity projectiles. For those inside, the results were far worse: every one of the would-be assassins was annihilated in seconds.

Long after Herron's gun had run dry, the fire from others continued, until finally a shot penetrated the fuel tank. The sedan exploded, jumping a foot off the ground, before settling on tireless axles, burning and spewing acrid smoke high into the air. Only then did the mix of cops and agents consider their job to be done, the gunfire easing and a silence descending on the scene.

Herron sighed. "That's a wrap."

"You can say that again…" Bradshaw replied. "Good driving."

Herron nodded, feeling a sense of camaraderie with Bradshaw for the first time. "Good shooting."

They watched quietly as the DNI and what remained of his security detail climbed out of his battered vehicle. The man they'd seen at the casino – the man in charge of America's intelligence functions – suddenly looked a hell of a lot older than he had fifteen minutes ago.

And his protective detail looked a hell of a lot more paranoid.

As the DNI's bodyguards trained their weapons on the cops, covering their protectee against the risk of another of the cops being a traitor, the old man started walking to the plane. But then the DNI turned and locked eyes with Herron.

Herron's hand moved, slowly and instinctively, toward his pistol. He had the vibe that this might be the end of the road for him, which would mean more bloodshed. Kearns was safe, the DNI was safe for now, and he'd done his best to foil the Chinese plot – he wouldn't think twice about a shootout now if it meant he got away.

"Easy…" Bradshaw said, as if sensing what was about to happen. "Wait and see what he wants before you do something that gets you killed."

Herron glanced at Bradshaw and made a split-second decision. He didn't think the team leader was talking shit, and he'd gained respect for the man in the last twenty-four hours. Knowing he was taking a chance in trusting someone, he moved his hand away from his gun.

The DNI, eyes still on him, waved for him to get aboard the plane.

"Well," Herron said. "This should be interesting..."

5

———

Herron sat back in his seat and closed his eyes as the plane left the runway and climbed into the sky. After being disarmed by the DNI's people, he and Bradshaw had boarded the plane and been ushered to separate cabins. He had expected to be joined by others, but soon after the pilot had announced they were preparing to take-off, so he'd buckled in and kicked back, enjoying the opportunity to relax for a moment or two.

"Strange life you've got, Mitch," he whispered to himself. "From being hunted by every intelligence agency on Earth to sharing a plane with their most powerful figure..."

The plane levelled out, and Herron opened his eyes at the sound of the cabin door opening. A crew member entered, with a decent-looking sandwich and a can of soda on a tray. He put it down in front of Herron, but made no comment or eye contact with the grimy operative he was serving. It made Herron wonder what *other* shady figures found their way onto this plane from time to time.

With a shrug, he dived into the catering – it was the best thing he'd eaten since landing back in the States and it disappeared within a few bites. But by the time he was halfway through the soda, he wondered if *anyone* was going to talk with him during the flight. Perhaps even tell him their destination...

He climbed to his feet, tried the door, found it was locked. That meant he was a prisoner, rather than a passenger, which changed the equation substantially. Looking around the cabin for anything he could use to escape or arm himself with, he found nothing except the six-seater conference table.

The best he could do was be ready when they came for him.

He picked up his plate and smashed it on the table. It shattered into a dozen pieces, and Herron selected the largest, a shard he could easily plunge into someone's throat. Knowing it would cut his hand too, he gripped it, pressed his back against the wall next to the door, and waited.

An hour later, when the door finally slid open again, he struck.

Herron burst into action, rounding into the doorframe and pushing the new arrival back against the wall of the plane, his left forearm pressing into the man's chest as his right brought the ceramic shard up to his throat. Beyond the door, several surprised agents reacted as fast as they could, and Herron quickly had several weapons trained on him. The man in his grasp, however, remained utterly unmoved.

"Nice to meet you, Mr Herron," he said, without a trace of fear. "I'm Mike Burgess, the Director of National Intelligence."

"Thanks for the sandwich," Herron replied.

"You're welcome," Burgess said. "Now that we're introduced, let me tell you this can go one of two ways. You can sit down to hear what I've got to say to you, or you can slice me open and be shot to death a split-second later."

Herron pressed the shard against Burgess' throat a little harder. "I'm happy to talk, but I'm *not* happy to be locked up. Got it?"

"Got it." Burgess gave a little smirk. "You've proven your loyalty and your worth, so you have my promise. No more being locked up in cages or rooms. Good enough?"

"You'll *also* remove the threat against Erica Kearns..."

"That I won't do, Mr Herron," Burgess said, his tone cold. "You've earned a small respite, but I'm not quite ready to surrender the initiative entirely, although Ms Kearns *has* slipped off the radar. You do have a history of biting the hand that feeds you. What I will do is reiterate my colleague's position: if you complete your assignments for us faithfully, no harm will come to your friend After all, she is an eminent scientist in service to the nation."

Erica slipped the net and got into hiding...
Good.

Herron considered a moment, then dropped his makeshift blade on the ground. He sat, and waited while Burgess did the same. "I want some answers."

"And you deserve some," Burgess replied, his demeanour much warmer now. "You've earned that much. Thank you for saving my life. We thought we'd vetted those cops."

"Tell me what we're up against and exactly what you want from me?"

Burgess gestured at one of his agents by the door, and a moment later, the Suit entered. He sat next to the DNI and the two men smiled at each other. Seeing them together for the first time, Herron noticed more than a passing physical resemblance between them.

"As you seem to have just figured out," Burgess said, registering Herron's expression, "This is my son, Reeve. He's an agent and handler with the CIA, but for the moment he's on special assignment to my office."

Herron nodded. "Because he's one of the few you can trust in the intelligence and special operations establishment, outside of Bradshaw and his team, and your own protective detail."

Burgess nodded. "He's *also* the one who had the bright idea of adding your expertise to our ranks. Without him you'd be a body floating in the Pacific right now."

Herron said nothing.

Burgess rubbed his hands together. "So, you deserve the truth, here it is. China is going full bore for Taiwan, hoping to catch the West off guard while dozens of countries are still focused on the changes in Hong Kong. The PRC's leadership is feverish about this aim, and the military is dutifully preparing to carry out the mission. Nobody in the White House or the State Department thinks a diplomatic solution is possible. We're on the cusp of a war..."

"Bradshaw told me all of that," Herron said, crossing his arms. "If that's all there is to it, then you've wasted your time and mine pulling me aboard this plane."

Burgess glared at Reeve, clearly unimpressed that his son's hand-selected operations leader had told Herron *anything*. "Very well. What you *don't* know – what *nobody* knows except my son and I – is that we have an asset who can stop the invasion cold, so long as we can meet with them in person and provide them the means to do so."

Herron raised an eyebrow. "So why not just do that?"

"Because the only person the asset will meet with is me." Burgess put his palms down flat on the table and leaned forward. "China knows there's a leak in their boat, a US asset in their midst. They also know I've been that asset's handler for three decades, but they *don't* know *who* the asset is. To stop the invasion, I need to get in a room with my asset. To stop that, the Chinese either need to kill me or expose my agent."

"That's why you were so intent on attending the meeting at the casino," Herron said. "Your asset was inside. You were hoping to use international meeting security meeting as a cover."

"Correct."

"Why not just send someone else to meet with the asset? Your son?"

"I have met my asset in person once a year for thirty years. They have made it clear that cannot change, even when I became Director of National Intelligence. If it were anyone else, I would have cut the line and let them float away years ago, but they are simply too valuable."

"Okay, so what's the plan?"

"I have one last chance to meet them, seven days from now in Washington D.C...." Burgess' voice trailed off. "I'm going to need your help to keep us both safe."

Herron nodded, seeming to take both Burgess and Reeve by surprise, as if they'd expected him to argue or make a scene. But he was happy to hear them out, learn all he could and perhaps use that to secure a better post-mission future than a bullet in the brain.

Leaning forward in his chair, Burgess explained what needed to be done. By the time he was finished, Herron's could only look at him, stunned.

"What you're asking me to do will start a war if it's uncovered," he said at last. "Regardless of what happens with China and Taiwan..."

"That's why we're using a deniable asset with a history of aggression against China," Burgess replied. "Besides, if I don't meet with my asset, war is one hundred percent certain."

The equation stacked up. It also gave Herron a glimpse of all some leverage. "I'll do it. If you agree to let me walk at the end of the mission."

"That wasn't the deal," Reeve said, speaking for the first time since he entered the cabin. "You agreed to help us in return for keeping your friend safe, then it was curtains for you once the job was done."

"You guys aren't as good at this as you think you are," Herron said with a grin. "My friend *is* safe – you said so yourself that you couldn't find her – so you'll need to come up with more motivation to get me off my ass."

"We could shoot you right here," Reeve said.

"You're going to do that at the end of the job anyway."

Herron sat back in his chair and folded his arms. He'd bet everything that they wanted his help more than they wanted him dead. But with each second that ticked by without an answer, he wondered if he'd actually overplayed his hand.

Burgess opened his mouth to speak... but was stopped by the boom of a gunshot. A second later, the plane dove. Herron and Burgess gripped the arms of their chairs, but Reeve was sent sprawling, cracking his head against the side of the table.

Herron climbed to his feet, the turbulence threatening to send *him* to the deck. "Stay here," he said to Burgess on the way past. "Lock the door, look after your son, and hope like hell one pilot is still alive."

He grabbed the piece of broken plate off the floor, then struggled out of the cabin. The agents stationed outside earlier were gone, no doubt investigating the gunfire for themselves; hugging the wall, Herron too made for the front end of the plane.

Although Burgess' protective detail had proven themselves, there was the chance other agents or crew aboard the plane had been turned as well. And if they got into the cockpit, or the locked room where he'd left Burgess and Reeve, then it could mean bad news.

"Stop!" Two of the agents from Burgess' protective detail who'd been stationed outside appeared in the passageway ahead, levelling pistols at Herron, his comrade doing the same thing. "You're meant to be in Cabin Four!"

"Which means you know I couldn't have been messing in the cockpit," Herron shot back at them urgently. The plane was losing altitude with each passing second, he didn't have time for this.

The agents looked at each other and reached the only logical conclusion. Neither showed any signs of panic, despite the gravity of the situation. Finally, one of the pair spoke. "We were just coming to secure Director Burgess."

"Do that, I'm going to try to stabilise the aircraft," Herron replied. He held out one hand, gripping a fixture on the wall with the other. "Gun!"

The two agents hesitated... then one slapped his pistol onto Herron's palm. "Don't make me regret this..."

"The only thing you'll regret is if I can't get this plane levelled out. Now go!"

He slipped the broken ceramic blade into his pocket and watched for a second as they headed off, hoping neither of *them* was a Chinese sleeper. But they'd already had a chance to take out Burgess in Vegas, so he had to trust them now. He'd have to play the odds that the pair of them were loyal.

At the front of the aircraft, several civilian servers were bashing on the door, begging the pilots to right the plane. Herron was shooing them aside, when several gunshots sounded. Three holes were blown in the door, and while none of them found him, one server took a shot and dropped to the floor screaming.

"Move!" Herron shouted, but the remaining cabin crew needed no more encouragement. Herron hit the deck as they scattered, then opened fire at the door.

His shots boomed inside the narrow space, bullets ricocheting into the wall as they bounced off the lock. He calculated the stray rounds were worth the risk: the plane was going to hit the dirt unless he could get into the cockpit quickly, and a gunshot wound was far more survivable than crashing in a jet. By aiming up at the lock he also hoped any penetrating shots would hit the ceiling beyond, and not the pilots or instrumentation.

The plane's angle of descent suddenly steepened, and leaping up, Herron burst forward and slammed into the door. He grunted as it gave way, and, in an instant, he summed up the situation beyond it.

It was close to the worst probable outcome: both pilots were dead, dumped unceremoniously on the ground. The rogue server who'd killed them may as well have been dead, bleeding out in a chair from one of Herron's stray rounds. And the plane had its nose pointed down, alarms wailing in the cockpit as it headed rapidly for mountains ahead.

He had maybe thirty seconds.

Herron put his last bullet into the head of the rogue server, ensuring he was no longer a threat. Then, ignoring the screaming alarms, he dropped into the pilot's seat. A decade and a half ago he'd had limited flight training, but he didn't need *any* experience to know flying into a mountain was bad business.

He gripped the stick and pulled back on it.

The nose of the aircraft lifted, the engines and flaps of the plane straining to prevent impact with the mountain.

Three seconds to impact, the top of the mountain dropped out of view of the windshield...

Two seconds to impact. Herron closed his eyes.

One second.

There was a deep rumbling sound as the bottom of the aircraft skimmed the mountain... then they were clear.

The alarms cut out, nothing but blue sky staring back at him. He sat back in the pilot's chair and groaned, knowing how close he'd come to death, how close a war between China and Taiwan had been. He hadn't yet figured out how he was going to *land* the plane, but that didn't seem to be the most overwhelming problem ahead of him.

With Chinese sleepers appearing like termites in a derelict house, getting the man in the same room as his asset seemed impossible.

He should start by checking the DNI was still safe. He located the autopilot and engaged it, his eyes roaming the cockpit controls for the intercom button... but before he found it, something wrapped around his throat from behind and pulled him back against the chair, choking him.

Herron bucked and fought, trying to free himself as the life was strangled out of him. He reached up, fingers finding the length of fabric choking him, but unable to work their way beneath it – whatever the material was, it was being pulled back so tight it may as well have been glued to his skin.

Years of training kicked in, dousing his panic; with no better options, he put his feet up on the instrument panel and pushed off, trying to wrest the chair free of its fastenings. He strained with all the strength in his legs, but as he'd feared the chair was too well anchored to the floor.

His lungs burned from the exertion and the lack of oxygen... if only he still had ammo in the pistol resting in his lap. Then his eyes widened as he remembered he had *another* weapon at his disposal, forgotten in the struggle to keep breathing.

Reaching into his pocket, he pulled out the plate shard he'd been relying on until the agent had given him the pistol.

Whoever was choking him – another rogue server? – must have registered the movement, because the fabric pulled back on his neck even harder, Herron's attacker grunting from the effort. Herron raised the shard to saw at the cloth just behind his ear, so he wouldn't cut his own throat. It wasn't very sharp, and he wasn't sure he'd get the job done in time, but he hacked away like his life depended on it.

Because it did.

His vision blurred, black spots flashing across it; he only had seconds left. His lungs were screaming, his heart pounding, his entire body drenched in sweat. He slashed and hacked, the shard digging into his palm, his neck, slippery in his grip from the blood... and at last the material gave way.

The assailant fell backwards as he lost purchase, and Herron gratefully sucked in air. He got to his feet, turned and saw another rogue server. Glad the server hadn't had a gun, Herron dived on top of him and drove the shard into the sleeper's exposed neck. It bit deep, the man's cry of pain becoming a gurgle as Herron twisted the blade in his throat.

Blood spewed from the wound as Herron bored into the man's neck, all the anger and adrenaline that his desperate struggle to survive had built up inside of him released in one brief, brutal act. It ripped through muscle and veins and – swiftly – the carotid artery, spraying the cockpit with blood, pumped out at high pressure.

Gradually the spurts grew weaker, the sleeper's

heart failing until what blood he had left could only drool onto the carpet.

Herron collapsed in the gore, chest heaving. Much as he wanted to lie there forever, he still had a plane to land, not to mention finding out if Burgess had survived yet another attempt on his life. He stood, trying not to slip in the blood, and made to leave the cockpit, now a high-tech a mausoleum filled with bodies.

He returned to the corridor, marching back in the direction of the cabin where he'd left Burgess. He didn't give a damn about hiding his weapon now, and he'd shoot anyone who got in his way, so enraged was he at the constant treachery.

The cabin door was open.

Leading with his pistol, Herron rounded the corner into the room and breathed a sigh of relief when he saw Burgess, Reeve, Bradshaw, and the other agents Herron had seen in the passageway. They all looked at Herron in surprise: he was cut, battered and drenched in the dead server's blood.

"What the hell happened up there?" Burgess asked. "We thought everything was okay when the plane levelled out."

"Turns out you had *two* servers who were on the Chinese payroll," Herron said.

"The pilots?" Reeve chimed in, then continued when Herron shook his head. "So who's flying the plane?"

"The auto pilot... let's call him Bob," Herron said. "Anyone know how to land us?"

Blank stares answered him.

"Fine, I *can* do it, but I *can't* guarantee we'll

survive..." Herron headed for the door, then turned back to the group as he had another thought. "And I'll need one of you to handle the air traffic permissions..."

6

———————

With Herron at the stick and Burgess using his immense power to bully air traffic controllers in Minneapolis, the DNI's jet was able to complete a passable – although not entirely flawless – landing. While Herron could happily never see the controls of a plane again, he'd got everyone down alive.

Now he just had to *keep* them that way.

Landing in Minnesota had been the first part of that effort. Any Chinese sleepers who remained would expect Burgess to head right for D.C., or a city along the path there. Instead, Herron had taken them north; from there, they'd take a slower – but safer – route to D.C. It wasn't a perfect plan, but it was the best he could manage, and it had got them on the ground without finding another welcoming party on the tarmac, ready to fill them with lead.

Standing in the plane's shadow, spared from the burning sun for the moment, Herron was holding court with Burgess and Reeve while Bradshaw found them a vehicle. The father-and-son pair were visibly shaken, and far less standoffish with Herron than before; clearly, they recognised that without his intervention, they'd most likely be dead now.

"So what do we so now?" Burgess asked. "I can get on the blower to D.C. and get some more agents to cover us while we head for the meeting..."

"That's not happening." Herron paused, letting the words sink in. "*None* of your people – nobody in the special forces and nobody working for any national security agency – can be trusted to escort you right now."

Burgess shook his head. "Totally ridiculous. Surely all the Chinese sleepers have taken their shot by now?"

"Are you prepared to gamble with your life? With starting a war?" Herron was met with silence. "Didn't think so. Bradshaw and I could have put a bullet in you already, so you know we're reliable. Nobody else is getting near you."

Reeve, at least, seemed convinced. "Okay, but how the hell do we get out of here? Anything we book through my father's office or my agency will show up on too many computers and be seen by too many eyes."

"You're right. And commercial flights are too risky. So we're going to do this the old-fashioned way." Herron smiled, as Bradshaw pulled up in a decades-old Ford sedan.

Burgess scoffed. "In *that*?"

"It's the only way I can be sure to get you there safely *and* alive. Now we've got a few thousand miles to cover, so it's time for you guys to get used to the idea that I'm in charge for the next few days..."

"What makes you so confident?" Burgess demanded.

"I've spent most of the last few years staying off the radar of intelligence agencies all around the world."

"That's not *technically* true... you were captu—"

"I was captured when I put my head above the parapet to mess with China's attempts to control other countries and fuck with innocent people," Herron said. "If I was the devil you all make me out to be, I'd still be on my boat."

His statement seemed to sink in, because neither Burgess nor Reeve argued about the plan any further. Instead, they followed Herron across the tarmac and into the beat-up old car, The minute they were inside – Herron riding shotgun and the two VIPs in the back – and the doors were closed, Bradshaw hit the gas, navigated out of the airport, and got them onto the interstate highway.

Herron stashed the pistol from the plane under his seat, then turned to Bradshaw. "Keep us five miles an hour below the speed limit and drive like you're a one-hundred-year-old, church-going grandmother."

Bradshaw nodded. "Okay."

Herron twisted in his seat to look at Burgess, who sat behind the driver. "If we avoid any random encounters with the cops, there should be no way for the Chinese sleepers to track you."

They drove in silence for several hours. At the wheel, Bradshaw complied with Herron's request, driving slowly and pulling over only for the occasional rest stop. Herron simply enjoyed the few moments of calm before the impending storm, staring out the window as the scenes whizzed by of a country to which he thought he'd never return.

His thoughts drifted to Erica Kearns. Although it had only been a day or so since they'd spoken, it felt like a lifetime. He'd survived a pair of shootouts, saved a plane from hijacking, and managed to convince both Burgess and Reeve that he was an ally rather than an enemy. He hoped she had also been hustling, getting somewhere off-grid so that she couldn't be found if Herron's situation shifted, putting her in danger once again.

For now, he had enough insurance against that to keep working with Burgess and Reeve.

* * *

He must have fallen asleep, because he woke with a start sometime later to find Bradshaw still at the wheel, but Reeve and Burgess snoring in the back. The afternoon sunshine had been replaced by the pitch black of night, the car's headlights the only thing brightening the road ahead as they chewed up the miles.

"Any trouble?" Herron asked.

"Nothing. You fell asleep. They fell asleep. I drove. Not much to report."

"Okay. Where are we?"

"Just outside Rockford, Illinois."

"We need to make a detour..."

As Herron explained his plan, Bradshaw smiled, then took them off the interstate. They were headed into Chicago, where Herron hoped to find another key thing they needed to get Burgess to D.C., arriving at an out-of-the-way industrial area just as Burgess stirred in the back.

"Does someone want to tell me where the *hell* we are?" the old man snapped, rubbing his eyes. "You're meant to be taking me to the meeting…"

"We are," Herron said. "But we need an insurance policy for when we get there. There's going to be Chinese agents, Chinese sleepers and who knows what else gunning for you and your asset."

"So how does stopping in the middle of a Rust Town industrial area help?" Reeve said, woken by the argument.

"Because in every good industrial area across America you can find a gun store with low, low prices…" Herron said as Bradshaw pulled over in front of a dimly lit store. "And, more importantly, with more relaxed standards of sale."

He climbed out of the car and headed for the gun shop, which occupied a stout-looking square brick building. There were bars on the windows, a faded sign up top, and a Confederate flag flying proudly from a pole on the corner. It had all the characteristics of a place Herron and Bradshaw might be able to get extra firepower without the pesky questions that normally accompanied such a transaction.

He walked through the door, Bradshaw following close behind. The chime drew the attention of the store assistant, who seemed surprised to see two guys who looked right out of an Army recruiting poster. The man moved his hands from the magazine he'd been perusing to under the counter. Herron knew exactly what he was reaching for, so he kept his own hands by his side.

"Evening," Herron said, approaching the counter. "My friend and I are just after some supplies."

"Strange time for it," the guy said, suspicion in his voice, although he had stopped reaching for his piece.

"We work night shift."

Herron and Bradshaw perused the shelves of high-quality hardware on offer. Herron skipped the rifles – too big and bulky for what they needed – and headed right for the pistols. He made a show of scrutinizing them, tut-tutting at each as he moved along the racks, making it clear he hadn't found what he was after. Elsewhere, Bradshaw did the same, his displeasure clearly audible.

They kept it up for a while, loudly discussing the specs of the guns on offer versus those they needed, putting on a show for the benefit of the shop assistant. They never once looked at the man, but Herron could *feel* him looking at them, which is exactly what he'd hoped for. To keep Burgess safe, they needed some special stock, and to purchase it with fewer questions asked than normal.

After a little more theatre, Herron caught Bradshaw's eye from the other side of the racks. "Want to get out of here?"

"Yeah," he replied. "Let's check out some other stores. We might get lucky there..."

"Sure thing." Herron turned and headed for the exit, Bradshaw close behind.

"Hey!"

Herron smiled, then turned towards the shop assistant. "Yeah?"

"I noticed you guys are... discerning," the man said, flashing a grin that was missing a few teeth. "I've got some specialist stock you might be interested in."

Herron looked at Bradshaw again, shrugged, then

headed back to the counter. This time, instead of reaching under the counter for a weapon to protect himself, the shop assistant came up with a large duffel bag. There was a heavy *thud* as he put it down and unzipped it. "Tell me exactly what you're after and I'll see if I can help you out."

"Small, concealed and powerful," Herron said.

"And off-books," Bradshaw added.

Bradshaw's words landed like an atomic bomb, lacking all tact and subtlety. The shop assistant's eyes narrowed and shifted between the two men, no doubt trying to figure out if they were cops or just plain stupid. Either way, he was now clearly closed for business, his hand moving to pull the bag back under the counter.

"What my friend is *trying* to say is that we'd appreciate discretion with our purchase," Herron said. "If a price can be paid for that…"

"Always." The shop assistant smirked. "But first I want to make sure you're not cops, so empty your pockets and lift your shirts."

Both men did as instructed. It didn't take Herron long – he had nothing in his pockets and he was wearing a t-shirt. It took Bradshaw a little more time, as he dropped a wallet and some keys on the table, but soon they'd satisfied the shop assistant that they didn't have guns, badges or wires. It wasn't a perfect foil if they *were* undercover cops, but it was clearly enough to tip the profit vs risk calculation in their favour.

"We have several firearms with… documentation problems," the shop assistant said. "Available at a premium price and paid in cash, of course."

"Of course," Herron replied. "My friend has enough

money in the car, but we wanted to see what you had to offer first."

The guy behind the counter finished unzipping the bag and held it open. Inside was about a dozen firearms of different types and conditions, promising firepower *and* discretion. Bradshaw dived in first, pulling out a compact machine pistol, while Herron chose another handgun to go with the one he had in the car.

"We'll take those," Herron said, putting the weapon on the counter. "We'll need enough ammo for a decent amount of work."

"Goes without saying," the shop assistant agreed. "That'll be a grand, non-negotiable."

Herron gestured for Bradshaw to get the cash from the vehicle. They'd withdrawn enough from an ATM right near the airport to cover their meals, accommodation and other expenses for the few days they'd spend in transit to D.C. It was a risk, because it would ping Burgess's location for anyone who was looking, but Herron had decided it was worthwhile, given they'd moved on quickly after that.

As the shop assistant went digging for ammo, Herron took a step back from the counter, listening hard. Gradually the tell-tale *thud thud thud* of a helicopter grew loud enough that he couldn't miss it, before coming so close to the gun store that the windows started to shake.

"Shit."

He ran to the front of the store and looked out. A police chopper was hovering overhead, its spotlight illuminating the beaten-up sedan that had carried them safely through multiple states. In the distance there was the wail of sirens, telling Herron had mere moments to act. He didn't know who – or what – had given them away, but he knew those cops were working for *someone* who wanted Burgess dead.

He turned back to the shop assistant. "Decision time, buddy. There's going to be a swarm of cops here in a minute. They're after me and my friends, but you can bet your ass they'll go through your store with a fine-tooth comb afterwards. So, you can either give me the bootleg weapons and avoid any curly questions, or wait until the cops find them..."

The man's eyes widened as he realised what that would mean for his store – and his freedom. Then, taking a step back from the bag, he just said, "Take them."

Herron stuffed what the ammo the shop assistant had found into the duffel bag, grabbed it and headed for the door. Outside, the intense glare of the chopper's spotlight had brought daylight to the parking lot, and Herron had to shield his eyes as he ran for the car, pleased to see Bradshaw had the engine running.

"Trunk!" Herron shouted over the noise of sirens and chopper blades. The second Bradshaw popped it open, he threw the bag of guns inside, and slammed it shut. A few seconds later, he was in his seat. "Go!"

The old sedan's engine roared as Bradshaw hit the gas, taking them back onto the road. The police chopper kept its spotlight on them, and Herron knew it'd be hard to shake the cops, but he had to trust Bradshaw to see to that. *His* priority was figuring out how the cops had found them.

He glared at Burgess and Reeve, playing a hunch. "Which one of you kept a phone?"

"Not me," Burgess said, then looked at his son. Reeve's expression was ashen. "Oh no. You didn't?"

"It's my personal phone, not an agency one. I—"

"You've put us all – no, you've put *the whole goddamn world* – in danger," Herron snarled. "Hand it over."

Reeve dug into his pocket and came out with the phone. The moment Herron had it in his hand, he wound down the window and tossed the device.

Reaching under the seat, his fingers snagged his pistol and he drew it clear. He didn't want to shoot it out with the cops; normally, he'd be loath to engage law enforcement officers who were just doing their job, but the stakes were too high. If Burgess was captured or killed, the war that followed could kill millions.

"Hope you've got a plan," Bradshaw said, now Herron's attention was back on the chase. "Because this rust bucket will not outrun a half-dozen police cruisers, never mind that chopper."

"It won't have to." Swiftly, Herron outlined an idea for him. "Follow the signs and I'll take care of the rest."

He sat back in his seat, letting Bradshaw focus on driving at top speed. Over the roar of the engine, he could still hear the sirens of the police cars encroaching on them, but Bradshaw was doing an admirable job of keeping them ahead of their pursuers. It was going to be a close call, but Herron's confidence that they'd be able to escape was growing with every mile.

He'd been to Chicago before, on an assignment for the Enclave. The mission had involved erasing a target while he ate dinner at a boating club on Lake Michigan it had gone flawlessly. But while he had scouted the location, Herron had noted the sheer number of expensive boats whose owners had keys left in the ignition. Back then, he'd filed the information away. Now he'd profit from it.

Bradshaw got them to boat club moments later, pulling the car to a screeching halt.

"Out!" Herron shouted at them, and everyone piled from the car and started running towards the boats. He lagged behind, taking precious seconds to get the bag of guns from the trunk, but then he sprinted as fast as he could after them, still lit up by the helicopter spotlight.

Herron caught up with them near the first line of boats: yachts large and small were bobbing gently in the water. "Everyone pick a boat. Whoever finds one with keys, shout out!"

Weighed down by the guns, Herron boarded one yacht, immediately heading for the wheelhouse. The door was locked, so he shattered the small window in the middle of the door with the butt of his pistol. After that, it was a simple matter to reach inside, unlock the door and open it. A second later, he was disappointed to find the owner hadn't just relied on a locked door for security – there were no keys in the ignition.

By splitting up the group, Herron had bought four tickets to win the yacht lottery, but they were still racing the clock: one of them would have to strike it lucky soon or the cops would catch them.

He ran from the boat, still hauling the guns, to see several police cruisers were now parked near their sedan, officers running to intercept them. Herron cursed and ran to the next yacht along, to find Bradshaw disembarking and shaking his head. Next in line – Reeve's assigned yacht – they busted again, but when they hit the yacht Burgess had boarded, they finally hit pay dirt.

"Keys in the ignition!" the DNI called out, a wide grin on his face.

As everyone jumped aboard, Herron called out to Bradshaw. "You're in charge of defences."

Without waiting for him to confirm the order, Herron left the guns with Bradshaw and headed for the wheelhouse, where he sparked the engine. He may not have had much practice piloting a plane, but he had plenty of recent experience piloting a yacht, and soon he had the boat moving from its berth. Ideally, he'd be doing it in the daytime, decreasing the risk of a collision in the dark of night, but the glare from the helicopter's spotlight gave him more than enough to see.

Bradshaw had distributed some guns to Reeve and Burgess – both ought to know how to use a weapon given their positions and experience – and they were hunkered down, taking cover from the cops, who were swarming toward the departing vessel with their weapons drawn. A second later, the question about whether they'd open fire was answered, as the cops lowered their weapons.

Herron grinned. Clearly, whichever Chinese agent was pulling the strings with the local P.D., they didn't have enough clout to issue a shoot-on-sight order.

He got them out onto open water as quickly as possible, leaving the cops far behind on the shore. The chopper followed, however, its spotlight beaming down on them.

"What are we going to do about that?" Bradshaw asked as he entered the wheelhouse.

"Nothing," Herron said, feeling the gaze of Burgess and Reeve on him. "In a few minutes we'll be over the state line, so the cops can't touch us."

"Won't the cops in Michigan just pick up the baton?" Burgess chimed in. "We'll need to make landfall somewhere, and they'll just intercept the yacht when we do."

Herron gave him a knowing look. "Not if we swim..."

7

———

Herron groaned with frustration as he shifted in the seat of a *different* car. He was cold and chafing in clothing that was still damp hours after they'd swum from their stolen yacht to the shore. Suddenly finding itself in Michigan, the chopper that had been buzzing them in Illinois could do little to stop them stealing a car and hitting the road, still soaked from their night-time swim.

Hours later, the elation they'd felt at foiling the latest attempt to kill Burgess had faded, and now they were all tired, soggy and irritable. They were close to D.C. – only a half hour out – but after crossing half the country it felt like each minute was taking an eternity. Conversation inside the car felt like a distant memory.

Staring out the window as they chewed up the miles, desperate for a shower and some clean clothes, Herron grew more tense the closer they got. There were more police on the streets than he would have expected – a *highly* visible presence on highways and intersections. He felt safe enough, because they couldn't stop and search cars without cause, but it was still more heat than he wanted.

"We need to know what's going on with all these cops," he said, finally breaking the silence. "Pull us over at the next gas station you see."

Bradshaw nodded and, a few minutes later, had the car was parked at a small suburban service station. While Reeve slept and Bradshaw filled the car, Herron led Burgess inside and paid for the fuel with some of the cash they had left. Then, when he'd gotten the change from the cashier, the two of them moved to the back of the store, where a single payphone sat – sad and unloved – in the corner.

Herron put the change atop the payphone, then fixed Burgess with a hard gaze. "Call whoever you trust who's high enough to get us the answers we need. Take no more than a minute."

"Like in the movies?" Burgess said. "I feel like I need a ticking clock to help build the drama, as the enemy agents desperately try to trace the call..."

"They'll trace the call almost instantly," Herron replied. "I just want to be long gone before they can get anyone here to bail us up."

Burgess lifted the payphone's handset, fed the coins into the machine, then dialled a number he knew by heart. After a moment or two, he spoke. "It's me."

From then on, Herron only heard one side of the conversation, but it was enough to get the gist: the American intelligence community had been critically compromised by the Chinese sleepers; many had been rooted out, but it was feared some remained; the intelligence chiefs of the Five Eyes countries continued to hold emergency talks about how to overcome the multiple breaches; and China was pulling out all stops to put Burgess in the ground.

No doubt about it: the rendezvous with the asset would be difficult.

When the minute was up, Herron tapped the back of his wrist to signify Burgess was out of time. The intelligence leader killed the call.

"That didn't sound good," Herron ventured.

"It wasn't..."

"And the cops?"

"A precaution – word has got around about the sleeper cells, so everyone is being extra careful."

"Okay, nut check time. Is there any chance someone in American intelligence knows the identity of your asset?"

Burgess took his time considering the question. If anyone in U.S. Intelligence knew of the asset, the effort to get him together with the DNI would be critically compromised. They'd still try, because there was simply no alternative, but Herron would prefer to know ahead of time if there was a chance of a Chinese ambush.

"I don't think so," Burgess said at last. "I've never knowingly shared the asset's identity with anyone."

"Good enough for me. Let's get back to the car and find a motel, because I'm dying to get out of these clothes."

By the time they got back to the car, Bradshaw was already back at the wheel and Reeve was still sleeping. They continued their drive into the heart of D.C. and the closer they got to the centre of the city, the more cops Herron saw. Now that Burgess had assured him nobody else knew the identity of the asset, however, his mind was more at ease.

They pulled into the parking lot of a motel Reeve knew. Herron didn't bothered to ask how, but it looked like the sort of place you might bring your mistress for a no-questions-asked good time: nice enough to be sure of clean sheets but run-down enough to be sure of no paper trail. Herron didn't much care anyway; it couldn't be worse than the house he'd shared with Bradshaw's squad for a night.

When they were parked, Herron sent Bradshaw on a search for supplies at a nearby shopping mall. Then, telling Burgess and Reeve to wait, he climbed out of the vehicle and headed for the motel's office, at one end of the long rectangular building that housed a dozen rooms. As he walked, he let his senses roam, but nothing about his surroundings registered as a threat.

He pushed the door open, headed inside the office, and waited while the bored-looking man behind the counter peeled his eyes away from his cell phone. "Any rooms?"

"Let me check," the staff member said, lazily tapping away at his computer to check on the number of vacancies, even though the near-empty parking lot suggested there would be plenty. "We have four rooms available. How many you need?"

"Two." Herron dug into his pocket, pulled out a thousand dollars of Bradshaw's money, and put it on the counter. "I assume that'll cover it?"

"Sure, I'll just need some details..."

Herron pulled out another hundred-dollar bill, setting it to the side of the other cash and locking eyes with the man behind the desk. "That's not going to work for me."

The cashier raised an eyebrow in curiosity, then

shrugged, pocketed the cash, and took the keys for the rooms from a rack on the wall. "Enjoy your stay."

Herron took the keys for both rooms and headed back to Burgess and Reeve, who were standing in the shadows and away from the road with the bag of guns at their feet.

Smart.

He gestured for them to follow, opened up open one of the rooms for them and hid half the guns from the bag under the bed. Then he locked the door and headed into the other room.

"Home sweet home," he said, tossing the bag with the rest of the guns on the bed. "Neither of you is to leave the room for any reason until we set off tomorrow, okay?"

Herron was a little surprised when they both simply nodded, two powerful men who clearly now recognised they were in his world. He had enough guns in this room to keep them safe, with the backup stash in the other room; they just had to wait while Bradshaw arrived with the *other* supplies they needed and they'd be all set. They could eat, have a shower, get changed, sleep and then set off in the morning to meet with the asset.

Herron flicked on the television and slumped onto the sofa while Burgess jumped in the shower and Reeve caught some zees. He wasn't surprised to find that nothing about their run in with the police had made the news, proving yet again that what was reported was barely a fraction of what was *really* happening in the world at any one time.

Some time later, a pair of headlights illuminated the room for a second, then cut out. Herron peeked through the curtains to confirm the new arrival was Bradshaw, then headed outside and waved him over. The burly special forces operator locked the car and walked to the room, hauling a bunch of bags filled with items.

"Any trouble?" Herron said.

"Not a thing."

Bradshaw laid out their haul on the bed not occupied by Reeve. He'd done a good job of getting clothing, hats and makeup that would help them mask their appearance, and he'd also purchased some burner phones that would make communication a little easier once they went to meet with the asset. Combined with the guns they had, it gave them more of a chance.

While they were inspecting the gear, Burgess emerged from his shower, having re-dressed in the clothes he'd been wearing since they set off from the airport. "Oh good, you're back," he said to Bradshaw. "We'd better get ready; the meeting with the asset is tonight."

"What do you mean *tonight*?" Herron snarled, loud enough to wake Reeve. "We're all exhausted and we only just got here. You said the meeting was tomorrow..."

"I lied," Burgess admitted. "I knew we'd only get one shot at this, so I wanted to leave the reveal until the very last moment. We're leaving in an hour."

"I don't like surprises, Burgess," Herron said. "We'll go to the meeting now because we have to, but if you deceive me again, I'll put a bullet in your head myself."

"If we pull off this meeting tonight, there won't be anything left to lie to you *about*," Burgess said. "Now I suggest you get ready."

Angrily, Herron turned back to the bed where

Bradshaw had laid out their supplies, and started to strip off down to his underwear. He felt the eyes of Burgess, Bradshaw and Reeve on him, or, more accurately, his collection of scars. It was a common reaction whenever someone saw Herron without clothes on. And if it intimidated them a little then so much the better.

He grabbed a razor and some shaving foam from the pile of gear, then headed to the bathroom while the others got started on their disguises. He filled the sink with warm water, and got to work on the stubble he'd accumulated over the last week or so; emerging clean shaven, he was ready for the stage makeup Bradshaw had purchased.

It had been a while since Herron had used any sort of makeup, but he was deft at doing so, thanks to his experience as a contract killer for the Enclave. A few times, he'd had to disguise himself heavily to get at or away from a target, and it only took him a few minutes to slightly alter his appearance. It wouldn't be much of a countermeasure against someone *really* scrutinising him, but it would fool anyone taking a passing glance.

He cleaned the sink and returned to the main room of the motel, where the others had changed their clothing. As Bradshaw filed into the bathroom to take his turn, Herron picked a simple outfit of jeans and a T-shirt. He kept his own shoes, but he topped off the look with some fake glasses and a baseball cap for a team Herron wasn't familiar with.

When he was done, he moved onto the weapons, inspecting the assortment in the bag from the gun store, looking for the pick of the litter. He formed three piles: the junk he wouldn't trust to fire properly, the basic pistols he could trust Reeve and Burgess to operate properly, and the better pistols and machine pistols for Bradshaw and himself.

After he'd finished sorting, Herron loaded one of the machine pistols, a small and easily concealable weapon. He only found two magazines for it in the bag, so he backed it up with a pistol that he slipped into the waistband of his pants. He stuffed the machine pistol and spare ammo into one of the grocery bags, then stepped back to let the others complete their preparations.

A few minutes later, they were ready. All of them were dressed in casual clothes, a stark difference from what Reeve and Burgess usually wore. They all had hats, and they all had at least a pistol concealed from sight; in the case of Bradshaw and Herron they had some heavier firepower as well. Given they'd managed to reach D.C. without attracting any attention, Herron hoped they could get Burgess to the meeting intact, but aimed to make sure of it.

"We need to stop that war and foil the Chinese Government operation, so getting Burgess to that meeting with his asset is the priority of everyone in this room," Herron said, looking around at each of them. "When we get to the park, Bradshaw and I will establish a perimeter. I want Reeve in closer, sitting on a park bench or something similar, the last line of defence while Burgess heads for the rendezvous point."

"I'll only need a few minutes at most," Burgess said. "Once I've told him what I need to, he'll depart very quickly."

At last they left the motel room and bundled into the car. With Bradshaw at the wheel, Herron riding shotgun, and the others in the back, they drove for fifteen minutes to a small residential park, with a children's playground, a scattering of trees, and a fountain in the middle of the park. At this time of night, it was deserted.

Of all the places he would have chosen for a clandestine meeting to determine the fate of millions, the park would be near the bottom of Herron's list. He'd have preferred somewhere built-up and crowded, where he could deliver Burgess to the meeting and hide their encounter amidst a crush of people oblivious to what they were involved in. But here, in total isolation, it was impossible to hide. There was barely anything that could be used for cover, very little lighting to reveal hidden threats, and no good escape route.

If the Chinese had caught wind of the meeting or picked up Burgess's trail, they'd be in a world of hurt.

"Do a lap," Herron said to Bradshaw. "I want to make sure there's nobody waiting to snatch Burgess."

As Bradshaw took the car on a slow, meandering loop around the park, Herron kept his eyes peeled for threats, but there was nothing to find. When they'd finished the lap, Bradshaw parked their vehicle and they all climbed out. But still something felt wrong.

It was merest suggestion from the deepest recesses of Herron's brain, a faint warning he'd nonetheless learned to trust over the years. The same feeling had saved him as many times as his martial skills had, telling him that although he couldn't see a threat, it didn't mean there wasn't one to be found. It also meant he needed to convince the others there was trouble on the basis of a hunch.

"Change of plan," Herron said, looking at Reeve.

"You're going to stay at the wheel in case things to go to shit. I want you to keep the engine running and be ready to drive us out of here."

"No way," Reeve said. "I'm going to be close to my father, just like we planned it all along…"

"Then there'll be no meeting," Herron said, resolute about the small change. "You need me more than I need you, and now I'm armed again you can't stop me from walking."

"Fine," Reeve said. "We'll do it your way. But if something happens to my father there'll be hell to pay."

If something happens to your father, it's likely we're all dead anyway and the world will be at war, pal.

Herron waited while Reeve climbed behind the wheel and started the car and kept the engine running, then he and Bradshaw led Burgess deeper into the park. A while later, Bradshaw peeled off, leaving Herron and Burgess approaching the fountain.

"Got your gun?" Herron spoke softly. "If anything goes down, you might need it."

"Son, I've done my time in the military and the intelligence service," Burgess said. "I may be old, but I can shoot."

"Good luck then."

Herron slipped away, leaving Burgess at the meeting point, and moving to the opposite end of the park to Bradshaw. Between them, they were each responsible for covering half the park, an impossible feat for two men against any serious foe. Carrying the bag with the machine pistol in it and keeping an eye on the time, he patrolled silently, knowing Bradshaw was doing the same.

Movement.

Herron crouched down low in the shadow of a tree as he watched a lone, small figure head towards the meeting point. The plastic grocery bag rustled softly as he drew the machine pistol from it and held the weapon by his side. It was impossible to know whether this was Burgess's contact or a would-be assassin, but the same instincts that told him the park was a wholly unsuitable place for a clandestine rendezvous told Herron *this* was the person Burgess had come here to meet with. His hunch was partially confirmed a few moments later when the mystery arrival walked under one of the few lampposts lighting the path; the new arrival wore a tan-coloured trenchcoat, as Burgess had said they would.

His small moment of relief didn't last long, however. The burner phone vibrated in his pocket – the call could only be from one of two people.

Herron pulled out the phone, his eyes still scanning the surroundings for any threat. "Yeah?"

"Movement!" Bradshaw said down the line. "I see a van, no plates, and six armed dudes just spewed out of it."

8

———

"Fuck," Herron muttered, spotting movement on the perimeter of *his* end of the park – shadows in the dark. "There might be more at this end as well."

"We need to abort." Bradshaw said, just as the first bursts of gunfire broke the serenity of the night.

"No way," Herron replied. "If Burgess and his contact die, a million people die with them. I won't have that on my conscience."

He killed the call and pocketed the phone, gripping his machine pistol and drawing his backup gun. Wishing he had night vision gear and some heavier metal, he kept low and moved to cut off the angle between the shadows he'd seen Burgess's location.

As the gunshots continued from the other side of the park, Herron's senses worked overtime to find the shooters on *his* side. They had a considerable numerical advantage, plus they were on the offensive; Herron and Bradshaw were being forced to defend themselves *and* a pair of easy targets, never a simple proposition.

He kept to the cover of trees as best he could, hoping Burgess and his asset had cut and run, having achieved what they needed to at the rendezvous. He couldn't bank on it though, so he kept moving, as desperate for a target as he was to avoid becoming one.

Then a target appeared, near to the path to the fountain: a figure dressed all in black, revealed only by a hint of ambient light from one of the few lamp posts. Herron stalked closer, took cover behind a tree, then popped out and fired a short burst from his machine pistol. His target dropped like a marionette with cut strings, falling to the grass and not getting up again.

Herron ducked back behind the tree as his shots were met with withering gunfire from the dead man's buddies; now they had spotted his muzzle flash, they knew his location. The squat, heavy tree soaked up the punishment, but at least some of the operatives would be peeling off to take him down. They'd flank him from both sides, catching him in enveloping fire that he didn't have a chance of escaping.

So Herron did the only thing he could. He reloaded the machine pistol with one of his two spare magazines...

... then he charged.

Bursting from cover, he ran straight ahead, zigging and zagging as he did. The man he'd dropped hadn't been wearing night-vision gear, and if his pals were the same, they were as blind as Herron. They'd be left shooting at a spot where they'd seen muzzle flash rather than a real target; they'd also be cautious about turning their aim too much as Herron got closer, lest they fire into their own ranks.

Herron had no such restriction. Sprinting toward

the fountain and ignoring the hot lead whizzing past him, he did his best to locate the enemy shooters the same way they had located him: by muzzle flashes. When he was close enough to be sure they wouldn't fire at him for fear of hitting their allies, he unleashed.

He sprayed and prayed with the machine pistol in his right hand and the pistol in his left, both weapons aimed in the general direction of the enemy. With he had no idea if he'd hit anyone, he dived to the ground and started commando crawling to the fountain.

He'd assumed the enemy operatives were in constant communication and well-trained enough not to fire into their own allies, but immediately shots boomed, followed by the shocked cries and screams of men cut down by close-quarters gunfire.

They were firing at each other.

Herron kept his head down, glad to have evened the odds a little.

The fountain was bathed in pale light from the lamp posts, enough that Herron could see Burgess lying on the ground.

His asset was nowhere to be seen at all.

Herron was forced to prioritise. Without the asset's identity, he couldn't be sure if the mysterious contact had escaped or been taken. He had to get their identity off Burgess, and he had no idea if the DNI would survive long enough for him to take out the attackers first. Which meant he had to get to the wounded intelligence chief.

Thinned out by their own crossfire, the attackers were finally communicating enough to get themselves sorted...but to Herron's surprise, they didn't resume their offensive. Instead, they started to retreat, a few of them in plain view under the lamps.

They must think their mission is completed.

Each of the shooters tended to a casualty on their way, dragging them – dead or alive – out of the conflict zone and back to their vans. No trace of who was responsible for the carnage in the park was to be left behind, no calling card that provided categoric proof of who had taken out one of the America's most senior government officials.

Their caution was the only thing that gave Herron and Bradshaw a chance.

As much as he wanted to fire at the stragglers, taking out the frustration at his failure on the enemy who'd caused it, doing so would once again reveal his position to the enemy. He had to keep his head down and live long enough to get to Burgess.

The footsteps of the shooters grew softer and the gunfire from the other side of the park gradually eased, until Herron could neither hear nor see any sign of the shooters. He gave it another thirty seconds all the same; no matter how desperately he wanted to get to Burgess, he didn't want his head blown off.

At last, he stalked through the darkness towards Burgess, hoping he'd waited long enough to see off the shooters.

He hadn't.

As he got closer to the fountain, exposing himself in the dim light, several rounds pounded into the trees around him.

They left a failsafe – someone to make sure no one lived to talk about what happened here.

He braced his back against the tree as more shots

slammed into the heavy trunk. He was pinned down again, but, this time, there was no team of shooters to fool into firing into each other, and no absolute darkness to shield his actions.

What he *did* have was an ally

Herron pulled out his phone and hit fast dial for Bradshaw.

"Got a problem here," he said. "I'm going to need some help."

Swiftly he explained what he wanted. It took a minute for Bradshaw to comply, but as soon as Herron heard the pop of gunfire off into the distance, he moved. Rounding the tree, he ran in the rough direction of the enemy, hoping his hunch had played off.

Bradshaw was firing blind at the failsafe operative, with no real idea where he was. The chances of him finding the concealed shooter were small, but he didn't need to *hit* the shooter to affect him.

The natural human reaction for even the most highly trained operative is to turn to face the direction of any fresh gunfire. Herron was banking on the shooter turning to assess the new threat; that then left it up to Herron to find the operative before they returned their attention to him again. It was a gamble, but no more than he'd taken earlier – the sort of try-or-die effort needed when a mission went to shit.

Breathing heavily, Herron glanced left and right, desperate to locate the failsafe. His night vision had been shot to shit by all the muzzle flashes and the dim light of the lampposts, forcing him to rely on his other senses.

He zeroed in on the *crunch* of someone stepping on fallen leaves under one of the park's giant trees.

Herron raised the machine pistol and sprayed, unloading the full magazine in the direction of the sound. There was a chance he could be tagging Bradshaw or some unlucky civilian on a late-night walk who'd taken shelter from the carnage, but the balance of probabilities was in his favour.

The weapon was empty in less than a second, thirty rounds of hope spitting out to destroy Herron's enemy.

Moving in close, he kept the pistol levelled as he searched for anyone who might have survived his barrage. A second later he found the operative that had almost bagged him. The man was on the ground, unmoving and not making a sound. Keeping his pistol trained on the man, Herron used the light from the cell phone to illuminate him.

The operative had taken several rounds to the face, but Herron could tell he was Chinese.

There was no point looking for identification; these guys were pros. They'd breached the park, disrupted the meeting, probably killed Burgess and likely bagged his asset too. If not for Bradshaw and Herron, their mission would have been a flawless success.

As it was, it was just a success.

All Herron could do now was see if he could salvage enough to fight another day.

There were police sirens in the distance now, getting ever louder as Herron ran to Burgess and assessed his condition. It wasn't good. The DNI had at least six gunshot wounds on different parts of his body, none instantly fatal but each leaking enough blood that they soon would be. Groaning in pain, the old man's eyes were flickering closed as shock set in, and Herron doubted he would last more than a minute, especially in the cold of the night. Trying to staunch the wounds would be futile.

Herron crouched down beside him. "I think your asset has been captured. I need a name."

It took Burgess a second to focus, his eyes staring up at the sky as Herron spoke. "What happened?"

"I need a name," Herron repeated. "Tell me who your contact is and I can still save lives. Stop the people who did this to you."

Again Burgess took a while to gather his thoughts, so long Herron thought he might have lost him. Then, with his last breath, he moaned, "Sheng Yu...."

"Shit," Herron said. He paused to mourn the man he'd shared the road with – although it felt like so much more than that – then wiped his prints off the machine pistol and put it in Burgess's hand. "Good shooting, bud."

It wouldn't fool the cops – not really – but anything that confused their investigation of the shootings would buy him more time. He and Bradshaw already faced hefty odds, so even the momentary distraction of the legions of law enforcement who'd be tasked to find the killers of a senior U.S. government official would be a win. Finding an unidentified Chinese wet asset with his face shot to shit wouldn't hurt either.

Except the activation of Chinese sleeper cells would ratchet up the tension between the U.S. and China more than ever.

Herron bolted in the direction of his vehicle, slowing only when his burner phone rang.

"I took down a couple of them," Bradshaw said without preamble. "But they took the bodies."

"Same," Herron replied. "Burgess bled out near the fountain."

"And you left him?"

"I did..." Bradshaw didn't respond, clearly wanting more of an explanation. "The cops are going to be here any minute. If they catch us, I'm dead and you're in prison. But if they find him at the fountain and a Chinese shooter nearby, it'll shift their attention to finding out where he's been and what he's been doing the last few days."

"Fine. Where are you?"

"Headed for Reeve and the car, and hoping he doesn't get jumpy and shoot my ass off."

Herron killed the call and covered the last of the distance to the vehicle. He was also dreading that he'd have to tell Reeve about the death of his old man. But when he arrived at the edge of the park, he sensed – and then saw – that something was wrong.

The car was there...

... riddled with bullets.

Herron ran over to the car as Bradshaw approached as well, quickly ascertaining that Reeve was dead at the wheel. He'd been sprayed by dozens of bullets, and a quick check of his pulse showed that any attempt to help him would be a futile waste of time.

"This went to shit." Bradshaw said, digesting the news of Reeve's death as he would any other battlefield development. He was still holding his weapons ready, and sporting some scrapes and bruises. "What do we do now?"

"We get back to the motel and figure out a plan," Herron said. "The cops are closing in, so we need to toss our weapons and split up. I'll meet you back there in an hour. If I don't make it, you need to find Sheng Yu."

"That the asset?"

Herron nodded.

They didn't delay any longer. Bradshaw sprinted off in one direction, Herron in the other, running away from the park like a fitness freak on a late-night jog through the city. Cop cars tore past him, lights and sirens working overtime, but none stopped to quiz him.

When he was far enough away from the scene and the torrent of cop cars had dried up, he slowed to a walk and caught his breath. Then, drawing the pistol from his waistband, he kept the gun concealed until a vehicle approached from the other direction. Herron looked left and right, making sure they were alone, then he stepped out on the road. With his pistol levelled at the driver, he held up his left palm facing outward, the universal sign for *stop or get your ass shot.*

The car slowed to a stop. The driver looked to be some sort of construction worker, a burly dude wearing a high-vis vest, looking tired after his night shift. Feeling a small pang of guilt – offset by the necessity and urgency of the situation – Herron kept the weapon trained on the man as he rounded the front of the car to the driver's side door.

He popped the door open. "I need your ride."

"Have it, buddy, it's a rental," the construction worker said, raising his hands. "Not worth my life."

Herron gestured with his chin for him to get out of the car, and the driver nodded and climbed out. Keeping his hands visible, he slowly backed away and headed for the sidewalk. Herron was thankful at least *this* had been easy; nothing else about the past few days had been.

He slammed the door and hit the gas, putting miles between himself and the park. When he'd been driving for five minutes, he pulled over onto the side of the road, exhaled loudly with frustration, then wiped his prints off the pistol. Climbing out of the car, he walked down an alley, throwing the pistol in a dumpster and putting the remaining ammo into a drain, then he returned to the vehicle and made his way to the motel.

He didn't quite know what to expect there – an army of cops, a team of Chinese shooters – but, when he arrived, the place looked just as it did when he'd left. It was a risk coming here, but he hoped the Chinese and all their sleepers would keep their heads down, assuming the asset was secured.

He drove past a few times, circling the block as he checked for signs of trouble, before parking a short walk away. After wiping his prints, he walked back the few blocks to find Bradshaw had arrived. It appeared he'd stolen a car rather than hijacked one, because the window in his ride was broken.

"Get inside," Herron said to him. "I'll be there in a moment. I've got something to take care of."

Bradshaw raised an eyebrow. "Now's not the time for sitting on my ass..."

"That's exactly what you'll do while I find Sheng Yu," Herron retorted. "Trust me."

"Fine," Bradshaw said, his tone suggesting it was just the opposite.

Herron watched him return to the room in which they'd prepared for their operation, then headed back to the motel office to find the same guy who'd checked him in. Immediately ensuring he had the man's attention, Herron put a few hundred bucks on the counter, then asked him to amend one key detail about their booking.

Satisfied he'd planted sufficient bait, he left the office and headed for the *second* room they'd booked, and the guns he'd stashed under the bed. He took a few minutes to shower, knowing his trap would take some time to attract its prey, but by the time he was towelling off he expected a knock on the door at any moment.

He sat on the bed, growing more and more impatient; each passing minute took the asset farther from him. He wasn't sure Sheng Yu was even alive, but if he was it was imperative Herron find her before the Chinese Government could interrogate her and find out how he planned to stop the invasion of Taiwan.

He dozed – exhausted after days on the road with little rest except for the odd nap – until a pounding on the door, hard and urgent shocked him back to full consciousness. He glanced at the clock and saw he'd been out for half an hour.

He grabbed his newly loaded pistol and pressed the barrel up against the door, roughly where the average person's midsection would be. Half-squeezing the trigger, he cracked open the door...then eased his finger pressure and lowered the weapon, despite the look of molten fury on the face of the woman outside.

"Good to see you, Zoe."

He'd last seen her a few weeks ago in Hong Kong, where she'd helped him escape the snare the Chinese Government had caught him in. Although he'd ultimately failed to stop them from taking Hong Kong, Herron's intervention had caused the Chinese

Government great embarrassment, revealing their systematic torture of prisoners in distant, barely known jails.

All Zoe would be thinking of, however, was that he'd rebuffed her efforts to help get him out of Hong Kong safely, in return for agreeing to work for the British Government. Now he'd called on her when he needed help – yet again – by registering the room under a name only she knew, raising all sorts of flags in MI6's monitoring systems.

"You've got a lot of fucking nerve shooting up that bat signal, Mitch." She pushed him in the chest, creating enough room to step inside the room. "You better have a damn good reason."

Herron said, closing the door behind them. "How about the entire American intelligence community being compromised?"

"That's not news," she said. "Why do you think all the Five Eyes nations have converged here? We're trying to find out who and what has been tainted, then we'll figure out how to put the pieces back together."

"And all the while China is making plans to move on Taiwan," Herron said. "I know how to stop them."

"You didn't stop them in Hong Kong," she replied. "I'm sorry, you don't deserve that."

"Sure I do. I couldn't get it done in Hong Kong, so I'm trying to atone by keeping Taiwan out of their mitts."

"Noble of you."

"Well, I didn't get much choice in the matter to start with." Gradually he filled her in on how he'd been captured and put into service via threats against Erica Kearns. "Despite all that, I actually *want* to stop this."

"Good luck with that. Their troop ships are loading as we speak and World War Three looks to be a near certainty." She sat on the bed. "Why am I here, Mitch?"

He sat next to her and gripped her hand, squeezing it as he dredged up a fond memory of the night they'd spent together in Hong Kong. "Because I need your help finding a Chinese Government official named Sheng Yu. I don't know anything about him, except the US Director of National Intelligence was his handler, and he said he could stop the invasion before it started."

"*Was* his handler?"

"Chinese agents took him out a couple of hours ago."

"Wait, Burgess is dead?" Zoe asked, eyes wide. "Why didn't you fucking *lead* with that? There's going to be an atom-bomb sized fallout from this..."

"No shit, but *that* war will be in the *shadows*: American spooks cutting up Chinese spooks in retaliation. I'm trying to prevent a hot war that kills millions."

"Fine," she said. "What do you need from me?"

"Every British agent you can mobilise, out there looking for a Sheng Yu."

"I can do that," Zoe said. "But I sense there's more..."

Herron held up his hands. "Well then I'm going to need your help getting to him."

9

Herron tapped his foot on the floor of the car, impatient for their target to emerge. They'd been waiting outside the Chinese Embassy in Washington D.C for hours, Bradshaw and Herron in one vehicle near the front gate, while the remaining four members of Bradshaw's team had paired off to cover other locations around it.

After luring Zoe to the motel and securing her help, Herron had been forced to wait while she worked her magic. Using MI6 intelligence assets, she'd quickly confirmed there'd been much chatter about Sheng Yu in the Chinese Embassy, centred on one member of staff who seemed *particularly* interested in Sheng Yu. The staff member, British intelligence believed, was the head of Chinese covert operations in the American capital, an attaché to the Ambassador named Ya Chen.

A senior representative of the Chinese Ministry of State Security in the United States, it was highly likely Ya Chen knew the specifics of the plot to activate

Chinese sleeper cells in the United States intelligence community. Hell, it was possible she was *behind* the plot, or had at least been involved in recruiting some of the sleepers. But, more importantly, she almost certainly knew the location of Sheng Yu, the only person with the power to stop the invasion and a person who China would do anything to silence.

Despite all their efforts, however, none of Zoe's assets had been able to find Sheng Yu, nor determine whether he was alive or dead. That frustrated Herron, but he knew without Zoe he'd have nothing at all, so he'd taken the information and thanked her for it. In return, she'd told him to forget seeing her... but to look her up again when he had some time to relax.

With that thought still fresh on his mind, Herron turned to Bradshaw. "This is taking too long."

"We could knock on the door?" Bradshaw snorted. In the driver's seat, he was feeling no less impatient than Herron. "Or fire a few shots in the air and see what happens?"

"No, I've had my fill of prison." Herron smirked. "Although sitting in a car with you over the past few days has been almost as bad."

Bradshaw held his hands wide. "You disapprove of empty coffee cups, greasy food wrappers and the stench of men with limited airflow?"

Herron laughed, the new laidback relationship he had built with Bradshaw making the surveillance a little easier.

Finally, a few minutes later, he nudged Bradshaw and pointed to the Embassy gate. "Movement."

The Chinese woman who had just emerged was

short, and sharply dressed in expensive-looking business attire – a blouse, a blazer, a black skirt and low heels. Even if Herron hadn't had a description of Ya Chen, he'd have guessed this was her. The guards on the gate couldn't have moved aside for her faster, and the pair of them had barely twitched in the few hours Herron had been watching them.

"We have eyes on target." Herron spoke his headset – another gift from Zoe – to the other members of the team, recently summoned to D.C. by Bradshaw. "She's left the main gate and is heading south. Get moving."

As confirmations came in from the other two vehicles, Bradshaw started their car and drove after the woman at a low speed. They passed her, letting one of the other vehicles in their posse pick up the trail, staying in communication the whole time. With one car dropping the target as another picked her up, they were likely to attract her attention than using one car or following on foot.

Ya Chen remained on foot, striding for block after block, her hands balled into fists and her arms swinging back and forth, powering her fast, determined walk. Only once did she low down, to make a quick call on her cell phone.

Herron wished he had the benefit of a signals intercept on her line. "Get me a little closer," he told Bradshaw. "Drop me off, and then you and your guys should all back off."

"No way that last bit happens..." Bradshaw said. He tapped on the gas a little, getting them closer before one of the other tail cars moved out. "You'll need backup if—"

"Fuck!" Herron ducked as the windshield shattered under the fury of dozens of bullets. Instinctively, he reached for the pistol he'd stashed under the passenger seat. "You hit?"

"No!" Bradshaw had ducked down as he'd slammed on the brakes. "She called in the cavalry and walked us right into an ambush!"

Herron popped the door and climbed out. Eyes wide and chest pounding, he stayed low, trying to get a bead on the attackers as he inched toward the engine block. As he scanned the road, he saw one of the other trailing cars had been riddled with bullets from three different directions.

Chances were good everyone inside was dead.

The engine block provided cover from at least one direction, giving him a chance to spot the shooters. They'd spilled out of a non-descript office building, and were now taking up covered firing positions between their targets and Ya Chen. Their aim would be to delay or kill Herron and Bradshaw while their charge got away.

It was highly coordinated moving and shooting, reminiscent of a first-tier group of operatives.

"Tanner, we're under fire, get your vehicle to the target right the hell now!" Bradshaw yelled over comms. "Anyone have eyes on the shooters or Ya Chen?"

"I do." Herron tried to keep his voice calm. "Ya Chen is continuing on her path – walking, not running – and there's around a half-dozen shooters clumped amongst some vehicles parked on the street."

Several shots pounded into the car, and a cry of pain from Bradshaw told Herron that his ally had caught one. Off into the distance, the wail of sirens could be heard, as D.C. police scrambled to the scene of the midday shootout.

They needed to end this fast or they'd lose Ya Chen *and* have cops to deal with.

"This is Herron," he said into the headset as more shots peppered his vehicle, the ferocity of the barrage making return fire impossible. "I need you guys to drive right into the shooters. I'll do the rest."

"You're crazy," one of Bradshaw's team came back.

"Maybe. But just do it."

Silence for a moment. "Roger that."

A few seconds later, Herron saw their vehicle careening at top speed down the street, right towards the cluster of cars Ya Chen's saviours had set up in and around. The shooters were slow to react, firing at Herron and Bradshaw instead of the new arrivals, shifting their aim too late...

Herron cried out in amazement as the speeding car slammed into the enemy cover, ping-ponging through the vehicles in a display of high-velocity carnage. Through all the smoke and metal, he saw at least two shooters caught in the wreckage, while the airbags had saved the lives of Bradshaw's people.

It wouldn't be much good unless Herron could neutralise the remaining shooters quickly.

He rose to his feet and strode out of cover, advancing on the Chinese interdiction team, chancing that the more proximate threat of the collision would hold the attention of his enemies. He fired his pistol at the first of the Chinese shooters, who was still dazed from the impact, hitting him twice in the chest.

To his surprise, he heard gunshots from the right of him, and turned to see Bradshaw was also on his feet and advancing. Between the pair of them, they poured fire into the stunned kill team, downing the remaining three members before they could regain their wits.

"You're hit," Herron said. There was blood on the big man's shirt, but the wound didn't appear to be slowing him down.

"Just a graze. Missed anything vital."

"You okay to stay here and mop up? I need to stay on her tail."

"Sure. I need to check in on my guys anyway," Bradshaw replied. "She really played us like a guitar."

"We haven't lost her yet." Herron reloaded his pistol. "Stay on the comms and be ready to move if I need you."

He broke into a run in the direction Ya Chen had been walking. She'd got the jump on them all, costing at least two of Bradshaw's team dearly, but that didn't mean she'd evaded them entirely. If Herron was anything, he was persistent, and he'd been blown off course plenty of times before in his career only to work his ass off and get back on track.

But he couldn't spot Ya Chen, even when, by his estimate, he should have caught up with her. She must have been smart enough to get off the road, go to ground in a store. It's what he would have done – hidden in plain sight until the heat died down.

Just as he was about to give up, his chest pounding from the exertion of his sprint, he spotted her, striding as confidently as she had been before the attack. This was a woman supremely confident ion herself; it seemed it hadn't even crossed her mind that her ambush might fail. He slowed to a walk, catching his breath, reverting to tracking her from a distance and hoping she hadn't figured out who he was.

"Target acquired," Herron spoke into his mic, wondering if Bradshaw was in cuffs by now. "What's the situation?"

"Two of my guys are dead, two are dazed from the collision," Bradshaw said. "What's your status?"

"In pursuit. She doesn't look overly panicked or urgent, which tells me she thinks she's clear of the attention for now."

"Do you need anything?"

"A ride," Herron said, giving his location. "Don't take too long."

He decided it was time to go loud. Driven by fury at the Chinese Government and anger at himself for not intercepting her right away – a decision that just cost two men their lives – he charged. He closed the distance rapidly, drawing his pistol when he got within twenty yards. Only then did she hear him, turning on the spot...

...just as Herron crash-tackled her to the ground, an irresistible force hitting a very moveable object.

He hit her as hard as a linebacker, driving his full force into her midriff, taking her down to the pavement in one brutal move. She hit her head, and lay there, stunned.

Several people around them squealed in alarm, as Herron jammed his pistol up under her chin. "Nice to meet you, Ya Chen. We're going to get to know one another *real* soon."

"Who *are* you?" Despite the crack on her head and the gun in her face, she showed no fear, although her eyes *did* widen as she finally recognised her assailant. "*You!*"

"Me."

"You're too late to stop the invasion," she said, sure of herself despite everything. "I now know all about Sheng Yu and his treason..."

"That may be true, but I'm going to find out all about you, as well," Herron said. "And I don't think you're going to find it a pleasant experience."

Keeping the pistol pressed against her, Herron stood and used his free hand to manhandle her to her feet. By now, some of the bystanders had started to organise, forming a loose ring of a half-dozen do-gooders. Herron didn't have the time or the patience to deal with them; he knew most wouldn't do anything to intervene, but he also knew there was one in every crowd...

Herron sensed the attack before he felt it, the arm snaking round his neck in a headlock. Still bruised from being garrotted on the plane, he winced in pain. As he was pulled back by the force of the attack, Ya Chen tried to break free of his grip and run, but Herron managed to keep hold of her. But he wouldn't be able to for long...

Moving fast, he used the pistol as a club, bringing it up over his head and slamming it into the do-gooder's skull. The headlock eased slightly, so Herron struck again and again, until the constriction around his neck vanished entirely. Still dragging Ya Chen with him, he turned to saw a burly guy on the ground, dazed from the pistol-whipping. He couldn't take a chance on anyone else in the crowd fixing for a fight.

He fired two shots into the air, and immediately the onlookers scattered.

Once again, Herron pressed the pistol against Ya

Chen's skull. "Our ride should be here any minute now, fresh off wiping out your spook buddies."

"You're too late. Your intelligence community is compromised as is your plan to stop the invasion. Our troops will be moving within hours."

"Then I guess we better speed things up. If you'd prefer to just *tell* me where Sheng Yu is and spare yourself the pain..."

"He's safe in Chinese custody," she smiled, despite the grave situation she found herself in. "Which is more than I can say about your Director of National Intelligence or his son..."

Herron's features darkened and he pistol-whipped her. A moment later, Bradshaw pulled up, and with the eyes of the bystanders still on them, the two men manhandled Ya Chen into the trunk and then slammed it shut. Their prisoner secure, Bradshaw re-took the wheel and Herron jumped in the shotgun seat.

"I hope your guys found us somewhere to lay low," Herron said. "Because we just committed about a dozen or so felonies..."

* * *

"Believe it or not," Herron said to Ya Chen, who was tied to a chair in the middle of a cavernous warehouse, "I was in your position only a few days ago."

"And how did you get out of it?" She raised an eyebrow, still showing no signs she was intimidated. "Agree to once again work for the government that wants you dead?"

"Yeah, but you've killed the guys I made the deal with, so I guess I'm a free agent." Herron shrugged.

"Good thing I'm happy to fuck with your government, which wants to kill millions of innocent people just trying to live their lives."

"If those millions of innocent people – and the governments supporting them – simply accepted the inevitability of the situation, everything would be a lot simpler."

"See, that's where we disagree," Herron replied. "You think Chinese control of Taiwan is inevitable. I think the only inevitable thing is right here."

He walked around to the back of the chair, tipped it onto its back legs, then dragged it – and Ya Chen – deeper into the warehouse, where a commercial freezer waited.

Bradshaw's crew had done a good job finding them a quiet place for the interrogation, perusing local real estate listings and coming up with an out-of-the-way warehouse for rent. Then they'd broken into the place and secured it until Herron and Bradshaw arrived. The airtight freezer was an unexpected bonus.

Herron dragged the chair inside it, then crouched down next to Ya Chen. "This is quite simple. If you tell me where Sheng Yu is being held, I stop the war and you'll live. If you don't, I beat the answer out of you, lock you in here and forget about you. One is an inconvenience for you, the other is certain death. This warehouse is empty and the next scheduled showing to potential tenants is four days away. You'll suffocate long before then."

Finally, she showed the flash of fear Herron had – honestly – expected to see in her quite a bit earlier. "You wouldn't dare murder the second most important

Chinese official at the embassy in Washington D.C. You'll start a war."

"Ah, but there's the beauty of it, you and your crew just murdered the Director of National Intelligence, and there's a body to prove it, so I don't think anyone in Washington will care one bit if you're found dead," Herron said. "Besides, there's a chance killing you will start a war, but if I don't get the information I need in the next few hours, the war will *certainly* start."

Herron stood and took a step back, his pistol held loosely by his side. He didn't want to lock this woman in a freezer and leave her for dead, but in the high-stakes game they both played, death was a constant risk, and it was a line-ball call whether or not she'd give him the information she wanted.

"The first Chinese troops will start moving on the island within the hour. You're too late."

"I've been told that before. But if that's true, there's no sense sacrificing your life over an inevitability."

That seemed to seal the deal for her, ending the easiest interrogation Herron had ever conducted. Hell, it had been harder *capturing* her than getting the answers out of her. A few minutes later, she'd revealed the location of Sheng Yu and given him enough detail about the place to give them a chance at a rescue – assuming he could trust her intel.

"Fifty-seven minutes until the first troops move in, by my count. You better hope we get to Sheng Yu in time."

He walked away and started closing the freezer door.

"Wait!" Ya Chen shouted. "You said you'd leave the door open!"

"No, I said, I'd stop a war and you'd live," he said. "So if the information is good, and if I succeed in getting to Sheng Yu and stopping the war, I'll call some cops to bail you out."

"And if you don't? If you die?"

"Better hope I don't."

Thirty-seven minutes to stop the invasion.

That's all that was left after Herron, Bradshaw and his two remaining men had driven to the four-storey concrete strip club to which Ya Chen had directed them. Bordered by a gymnasium on one side and an apartment building on the other, the club had one entry adjacent to the main road, guarded by two suited goons with discernible handgun bulges under their jackets. An alley to the left of the building offered the possibility of another entry option.

"Tough nut to crack for four of us armed with just pistols," Bradshaw said. "We're sure to find more dudes and more heavy metal inside."

"Not to mention an unknown number of civilians, half of whom will be tanked and getting in the way." Herron added. "Plus we don't even know if Sheng Yu is still alive."

"Or if she's in there at all," one of Bradshaw's guys said from the back. "Ya Chen could have been talking shit, and walking us right into a confrontation with private security. And that will mean cops too."

Herron thought that over for a minute, the words giving him an idea. "We don't have a choice but to go in, but we *do* have a choice about *how*."

"Well I'm not seeing a way inside that doesn't leave us looking like a bug hitting a windshield," Bradshaw said.

"I do," Herron said, then explained his plan. When he was done, he looked back at the two operatives in the back. "Good to go?"

Bradshaw's men nodded and climbed out of the car. After crossing the street, they walked along the sidewalk the short distance to the front entry of the club. The two guys on the door looked them up and down, then searched them, then let them inside. They clearly hadn't made them as anyone who'd been involved in the efforts to protect Burgess or Sheng Yu. Herron and Bradshaw might not be as anonymous.

Once the two moles were safely ensconced inside the strip club, they were to search the joint for any sign of Sheng Yu and do a headcount of the hostiles Herron and Bradshaw would face. Without weapons, they weren't to act until Herron and Bradshaw were inside and able to arm them both again.

That was the harder part. The armed goons at the door wouldn't let Herron and Bradshaw past without a quick frisk, assuming they didn't recognise them straight away.

The plan was to move the doormen away from their posts long enough to enter while armed. Simply shooting them in the head on the way past was an option – one he'd pursue if necessary – but Herron was hoping a little sleight of hand might avoid that.

He pulled out his burner, dialled 911, then put the phone to his ear. When the operator asked which emergency service he required, Herron said, "Police."

"What's the situation, sir?"

"There's been a shooting," Herron said, and gave the address. "There's more guys with guns. I think you need to send help right away."

The conversation continued for another minute – precious Herron hated losing – as the operator asked him questions. Then, finally, the operator was satisfied of the need to send police to the scene.

Herron ended the call and checked the time on the phone. He hoped the cops wouldn't take too long; there were now only a few minutes to get to Sheng Yu and do what was needed to prevent the invasion.

He sat back in the seat and waited. A minute later, there was the squeal of sirens off into the distance, then four police cruisers screamed down the street – two from either direction – pulling to a stop outside the strip club. The two goons on the door became visibly nervous as cops spewed out of the vehicles. Instinct had the doormen reaching inside their coats for their weapons, so highly strung were they about the capture of Sheng Yu.

Four of the cops took notice of this, shouting at the doormen to freeze and moving in closer with their own weapons drawn. All the while, their colleagues – another four cops – headed next door in response to the 911 call. They'd find nothing out of the usual, but it'd take them an hour or so to figure that out – more time than Herron needed. And, in the meantime, they'd be keeping the guys on the door busy.

"Let's go," he said.

He popped open the door, climbed out of the vehicle and started across the street. The doormen were up against the hood of one of the police cruisers and in the process of being frisked and cuffed; Herron and Bradshaw strolled right on by and through the now unguarded door.

They paid the entry fee to the woman manning the desk inside, who was more interested in peering out to see what was happening in the street. Passing through a set of curtains, they headed into the club proper, where loud, pounding bass from the up-tempo dance music had drowned out the sound of sirens, the large number of patrons inside the club oblivious to the cops rolling up in force.

Life went on in the club's own little ecosystem. Several dancers gyrated on raised stages in nothing but their thongs, getting up close and personal to the guys who were sitting in front and stuffing dollar bills into their underwear. On the floor, several more dancers roamed, trying to find willing patrons.

Herron's eyes skimmed it all, disinterested, until he spotted one of his team. He tapped Bradshaw on the shoulder and they headed over to their colleague, who was seated at a high-top table, an untouched beer in front of him. As they crossed the room, he spotted Bradshaw's *other* man at the end of the bar, where he could keep an eye on the entire room.

When they were close enough, Herron spoke into the ear of his seated ally. "We've got around twenty minutes. What's the situation?"

Bradshaw's man leaned in to Herron's ear. "Three armed guys on the floor that I can see, but there might be more. They seem focused on protecting *that* door..."

Herron's eyes shifted to where his colleague gestured with his chin: a non-descript door off to the side of the stage, where two of the three armed goons he had identified stood guard. As Herron watched no dancer went in or came out; something *else* was behind the mystery door. Absent of the context provided by Ya Chen, he'd assume it was management, but he was hoping for more.

"I need you to peel off those two guards," Herron said to the team member. "And tell your buddy to take care of the guard on the floor."

"How? If they decide to throw down, neither of us are armed."

Herron reached inside his waistband for one of the two pistols he was carrying. Trying to be subtle, he handed it over. "Do whatever you need to keep them busy and off our ass."

The order given and a rough plan of attack figured out, Bradshaw's man walked over to his colleague at the bar. They both looked at Herron and nodded. A second later, they were walking past on their way to the mystery door.

"Here goes nothing," Herron said.

He stood and started walking, even as the man he'd briefed took a swing at one of the goons on the door. It only took one: his sucker punch sent the thug to the ground. Few people in the club noticed the commotion right away, distracted by the music and the bare flesh, but the key person Herron had wanted to notice did: the *other* guy at the door gave chase as Herron's team member ran away.

Bradshaw stuck his foot out to trip the other goon. The man stumbled, hitting his head on the side of a table, knocking himself out.

On the other side of the room, the third and final guard started to move toward the conflict. His frown was a contrast to the enraptured leers on the faces of the other men in the club, ignorant of what was playing out around them. Even those who had seen the punch and the trip didn't seem to care much, moving away to give the security man space.

The guard froze as Bradshaw's *other* man – who'd been watching the room disinterestedly from the bar – approached from the side and jammed a pistol into his ribs. The two shared a few words, and the guard was escorted meekly away.

Herron leaned in close so Bradshaw could hear him, but he still had to yell. "Keep everything here under control."

Quickly moving to the door, he tried the handle and found it locked. Up close now, he could see card reader on the wall; a quick search of the unconscious man at his feet produced a pistol and an access card. He beeped it against the reader, pocketed it, and stepped inside.

With the door closed behind him, most of the volume was immediately drowned out. Away from the public eye, he kept the stolen pistol in one hand and drew his own with the other, each now capable of delivering death. And, although he was still conscious of running into civilians, he considered the possibility far less likely given how heavily the door had been guarded.

There was *something* down this corridor the people who ran the joint wanted hidden from staff and patrons.

He glanced at the time: a quarter-hour remaining. Stalking down the hallway he saw several doors on either side, and was careful to clear each as he passed. None held any threats, instead filled with the paraphernalia necessary to run a strip club – boxes of booze, snacks, costumes and odd stick of furniture. Finding nothing, he was left with just one door up ahead.

Herron tried the handle. Locked... but this time there was no card reader to admit him.

He looked up, confirming – and glad – there was no security camera, or else he might already be dodging bullets. The lax security gave him a chance, and he pounded on the door with the butt of the pistol. Standing back, he waited for what seemed like a lifetime. Finally, the door opened just a crack.

A Chinese man scowled at him through the gap. "Who are you?"

Herron answered the question by jamming his foot in the gap and firing his pistol into the man's face. He pushed forward, using his size to get through the door despite the weight of the dead man now blocking it. It seemed a little unnecessary, but Herron's training was never to leave potential hostiles in his wake, so he put another round into the man's head, just to be sure.

The room wasn't large, but there was plenty going on inside. There was a kitchenette cluttered with the mess of a half-dozen men who didn't give enough of a damn to keep it clean, and a mattress in the corner of the room with a bloody, unmoving figure laying atop it. He figured that was Sheng Yu, but he didn't have time to confirm it: several sofas were arrayed around a large flatscreen television, and the four thugs sitting on them were jumping to their feet and reaching for their guns.

"Weapons down, guys!" Herron shouted, aiming his pair of pistols. "Or I—"

He had to fire even before he finished speaking, unloading two shots into a man who had almost completely raised his weapon. At that point, Herron figured it was game on. He took a step back, downing another thug as he did so, then sheltered behind the door as return fire boomed at him in response. The heavy steel door protected him from the shots, but now he was pinned down and had lost the benefit of surprise. He had no spare ammunition for the pistols and the clock was still ticking.

Herron could usually get a clean kill through good intelligence, planning and tactical acumen; even when he couldn't, superior martial skill usually gave him an edge in a firefight. But at close range against two armed foes and with no cover, he was forced to buck that trend.

Nothing else would get the job done.

Bursting from cover, aiming where he thought the Chinese goons would be.

One was, firing at the same time as Herron, their pistols cracking in the enclosed space. Herron winced as a bullet whizzed past his head, close enough that he could feel the displacement of the air. In return, he drilled the shooter in each of his eyes, textbook-perfect shots.

The second shooter was nowhere to be seen.

Herron kept his pistol raised, searching for a target with his pistol. The last man he *had* to be behind the couch, so instead of advancing into an ambush, he simply emptied his clip into the sofa. Tossing the empty weapon on the ground, Herron advanced and confirmed the coward had been dealt with, a half-dozen holes in him.

Herron took possession of the man's gun, put a round in his head, then walked over to the door and locked it. Finally alone and secure in the room with the bloody – and possibly dead – figure on the mattress, Herron hoped he was finally where he needed to be.

He made for the mattress and assessed the person atop it. It was a Chinese man, about thirty-five, broadly the same height and weight as the person Herron had seen Burgess meet in the park. He wasn't sure, but it was a good bet that Herron was looking at Sheng Yu.

Sporting cuts, burns and bruises, it was clear the asset had been tortured – quickly and brutally. Whether his interrogators had got what they wanted or not they'd left him be at last, perhaps confident that the invasion was imminent and unstoppable.

But Herron had disrupted that... he just hoped Sheng Yu was still able to talk.

"Hey, buddy," Herron said, squeezing the man's arm. "I need you to tell me how to stop the Chinese invasion of Taiwan..."

Weakly, Sheng Yu opened his eyes, his gaze distant. "Told you... don't know anything..."

"I'm not one of the guys who has been torturing you, pal," Herron cut in. "We're almost out of time, Burgess sacrificed his life, so I need answers."

Sheng Yu focused his eyes on Herron, a feat that seemed to require Herculean effort. "American?"

"I am," Herron said. "And you don't have to worry any more about the men who've been torturing you."

"You know... Burgess?"

"I've been working with him to find you and stop the invasion. He and his son died in the park, but we don't need to let his sacrifice be wasted..."

"Need...a phone," Sheng Yu said. "Don't have... much time."

Herron pulled out his burner. As it lit up, he saw he had a bunch of missed calls from Bradshaw – he hoped they still things under control out on the main floor of the club. "Okay, what now?"

"Call... this number," Sheng Yu said, then slowly recited the digits from memory. "Put it on... speaker."

A second later, the call was answered by a male voice in Mandarin. Whatever he said was short and clipped, and made Sheng Yu to tense, despite his battered body.

"What did he say? Quickly!"

"Attack already underway... the first rockets launched..." Sheng Yu closed his eyes. "Too late..."

"No!" Herron said, and slapped Sheng Yu until he opened his eyes again. "You're not dying until we've pulled this off. How did you plan to stop the invasion?"

"Man on phone... member of Chinese space program..." Sheng Yu's voice trailed off and he coughed. "Can upload code...cripple China's satellites...its comms..."

"Causing chaos for targeting systems, communications and aircraft," Herron murmured. "It'll bring the Chinese military to its knees."

"More..." Sheng Yu coughed again. "Bring Chinese *society* to its knees... can take down... the Great Firewall of China."

"The thing they use to censor the population?"

Herron imagined the chaos it would cause for the regime. "Do it. Do it now."

Sheng Yu nodded feebly and, in his halting, pained voice, gave the man on the other end of the line his orders. They may not be able to save Taiwan but if they acted quickly enough he could prevent all-out war.

"You can... end call... it's done..." Sheng Yu coughed. "Military systems will go first... then civilian ones... then the firewall..."

"Thank you," Herron said. "Now let me get you out of here, find you some medical help."

"No point," Sheng Yu said. "I'm a... prominent businessman living in the United States... now they know about my treason... I'm dead."

"Then we can inform the U.S. Government of the service you provided and *they* can keep you safe. You don't need to die here."

"Yes. I do. I've known all along... twenty years... working with Burgess... a death sentence if discovered... now the PRC... will kill my family."

Herron cursed. After working so hard to get to this man, but the thought of leaving him to die stung. Just as he had with Erica Kearns so many years ago now, Herron felt a debt to this man – he wouldn't force the man to go to a hospital and into witness protection if the cost was his family.

But there might be a solution for that.

"I'll protect your family," he said. "Give me their address here in the States, then we'll get you some medical care, and I'll keep your family safe until you arrive. Then you can all go into hiding."

Sheng Yu was silent for what seemed like forever,

the offer turning over in his pain-fogged mind. "Okay... help me up..."

As Herron did so, Sheng Yu gave him all the details he'd need: wife, three kids, home address not too far from here. Having committed all the detail to memory, Herron walked Sheng Yu back out to the club. Bradshaw had all the patrons and staff up against the wall, being watched over by the other two members of his team. Every cell phone in the place was on the stage – nobody outside the club would know what was happening.

"It's done," Herron said. "I need you to call this man an ambulance and organise U.S. Government protection for him while he's in hospital."

"Can do," Bradshaw said, and pulled his phone out of his pocket. As he lit up the screen, he took a second to check something, then grinned. "Whatever you guys did worked. Chinese military comms channels are going nuts."

"They should be. We took out their eyes, their ears and their brains." Herron smiled wearily. "If it doesn't stop the attack, we still we helped the home team immensely. It might even drive the population to rise up."

"Sounds good to me," Bradshaw said. "I'll have some explaining to do about all this, but I was on Burgess's orders, so I should have official cover."

"Lucky you. Everyone who knew about my role in this and the deal I made is dead, so I'm going to sneak out while I've still got the chance. I have to keep Sheng Yu's family safe until he's well enough to pack them up."

Herron held out a hand to Bradshaw. They shook, and their partnership was at an end. Like so many other times in his career and then his life on the run, Herron was forced to turn his back on a man who'd become a brother over the past few days, someone he'd now trust totally to protect his back. Some people, like Kearns and Zoe drifted back into his life; others he never saw again.

The only constants he had were death and the need to keep moving.

ABOUT THE AUTHOR

Steve P. Vincent is the USA Today Bestselling Author of the Jack Emery and Mitch Herron conspiracy thrillers, and the Frontier Saga science fiction series.

Steve has a degree in political science, a thesis on global terrorism, a decade as a policy advisor and training from the FBI and Australian Army in his conspiracy kit bag.

When he's not writing, Steve enjoys whisky, sports and travel.

You can contact Steve at all the usual places:

stevepvincent.com

steve@stevepvincent.com

www.ingramcontent.com/pod-product-compliance
Lightning Source LLC
Chambersburg PA
CBHW030414120726
47904CB00007B/2267